Missing by the Sea

by

Kathi Daley

I want to thank the very talented Jessica Fischer for the cover art.

I so appreciate Bruce Curran, who is always ready and willing to answer my cyber questions; Jayme Maness for helping out with the book clubs; and Peggy Hyndman for helping sleuth out those pesky typos.

And, of course, thanks to the readers and bloggers in my life, who make doing what I do possible.

Thank you to Randy Ladenheim-Gil for the editing.

And finally, I want to thank my husband Ken for allowing me time to write by taking care of everything else.

Books by Kathi Daley

Come for the murder, stay for the romance

Zoe Donovan Cozy Mystery:

Halloween Hijinks
The Trouble With Turkeys
Christmas Crazy
Cupid's Curse
Big Bunny Bump-off
Beach Blanket Barbie
Maui Madness
Derby Divas
Haunted Hamlet
Turkeys, Tuxes, and Tabbies
Christmas Cozy
Alaskan Alliance
Matrimony Meltdown
Soul Surrender
Heavenly Honeymoon
Hopscotch Homicide
Ghostly Graveyard
Santa Sleuth
Shamrock Shenanigans
Kitten Kaboodle
Costume Catastrophe
Candy Cane Caper
Holiday Hangover
Easter Escapade
Camp Carter
Trick or Treason
Reindeer Roundup
Hippity Hoppity Homicide

Firework Fiasco
Henderson House
Holiday Hostage – *December 2018*

Zimmerman Academy The New Normal
Zimmerman Academy New Beginnings
Ashton Falls Cozy Cookbook

Tj Jensen Paradise Lake Mysteries by Henery Press:

Pumpkins in Paradise
Snowmen in Paradise
Bikinis in Paradise
Christmas in Paradise
Puppies in Paradise
Halloween in Paradise
Treasure in Paradise
Fireworks in Paradise
Beaches in Paradise
Turkeys in Paradise – *fall 2019*

Whales and Tails Cozy Mystery:

Romeow and Juliet
The Mad Catter
Grimm's Furry Tail
Much Ado About Felines
Legend of Tabby Hollow
Cat of Christmas Past
A Tale of Two Tabbies
The Great Catsby
Count Catula
The Cat of Christmas Present

A Winter's Tail
The Taming of the Tabby
Frankencat
The Cat of Christmas Future
Farewell to Felines
A Whisker in Time
The Catsgiving Feast – *November 2018*

Writers' Retreat Mystery:
First Case
Second Look
Third Strike
Fourth Victim
Fifth Night
Sixth Cabin
Seventh Chapter

Rescue Alaska Paranormal Mystery:
Finding Justice
Finding Answers
Finding Courage
Finding Christmas – *December 2018*

A Tess and Tilly Mystery:
The Christmas Letter
The Valentine Mystery
The Mother's Day Mishap
The Halloween House
The Thanksgiving Trip – *October 2018*

Haunting by the Sea:

Homecoming by the Sea
Secrets by the Sea
Missing by the Sea
Christmas by the Sea – *December 2018*

Sand and Sea Hawaiian Mystery:

Murder at Dolphin Bay
Murder at Sunrise Beach
Murder at the Witching Hour
Murder at Christmas
Murder at Turtle Cove
Murder at Water's Edge
Murder at Midnight

Seacliff High Mystery:

The Secret
The Curse
The Relic
The Conspiracy
The Grudge
The Shadow
The Haunting

Road to Christmas Romance:

Road to Christmas Past

Chapter 1

Sunday, October 21

Life, I decided, was perfect. A sunny day, good friends, crisp weather, and an autumn forest brilliant with red, yellow, and even a hint of orange. Yes, I realized, as I walked across a rickety wooden bridge that spanned the river fed by the nearby falls beside my best friends, Mackenzie Reynolds and Trevor Johnson, life, in that moment, was exactly as I had always known it should be. Not that my life in New York City, where I'd lived until four months ago, hadn't been wonderful. It was just that after years of feeling torn between two worlds, I finally felt settled. Returning to Cutter's Cove, Oregon, the quaint seaside town where I'd lived for two years as a teenager while in witness protection, hadn't been part of my original plan, but when the death of a friend brought me back, I knew I'd never be able to leave.

"Oh look," Mac whispered as we neared the end of the swaying bridge.

I looked where she was pointing, at a doe and her fawn. They looked up and seemed to have sensed our presence yet hadn't run away. "They're beautiful," I replied in a soft voice, so as not to scare them. "I wish I had my camera." The red from the vine maples entwined with the yellow from the aspens against the evergreen of the forest presented the perfect backdrop for the deer perfectly framed in front of the lazy autumn waterfall.

"Maybe you can get a shot with your phone," Trevor suggested.

I decided to do what I could with that, but I knew the shot I really wanted to capture could only be realized with the lens and filters I'd decided I didn't want to carry on the short but steep hike up to the waterfall. I'd always enjoyed photography, but after moving back to Cutter's Cove, I'd decided to turn my hobby into a career by combining my work in graphic arts with the photographs I spent a good part of each week capturing.

"If the shot works out, I'd love to blow it up and hang it on the wall in my office," Mac said. Mac had moved into the oceanfront mansion my mother had gifted to me when I decided to make the move to the West Coast permanent. She had previously worked for a tech firm in California but had decided to take a risk and start her own company. Currently, she ran that company from her office on the third floor of my house.

I snapped the shot and then looked around. "Did anyone see where Sunny went?"

Sunny was one of the two dogs who lived with Mac and me, the other my German shepherd, Tucker. I hadn't wanted the dogs to scare the deer, so I'd made sure they stayed behind us. Tucker continued to wait in the exact spot where I'd told him to, but the much younger and not always obedient golden retriever I'd found on the side of the road and adopted appeared to have wandered off. I hated to scare the deer, which I knew would happen if I called for Sunny, but I didn't want to lose her in unfamiliar woods either.

"Sunny," I called after angling myself away from the deer.

My summons was met with barking.

"Sounds likes she doubled back and took the river path toward the falls," Trevor said.

I looked back to where the deer had been drinking to find them gone. "I'll get her." I turned around and headed back along the wooden bridge in the direction in which we'd just come. "Sunny," I called again. I was surprised she hadn't come when I'd called her the first time. She tended to become distracted at times, but it wasn't like her to completely ignore a command.

Once I arrived at the point where one could choose to take the wooden bridge or the narrow river trail, I headed along the river. I could hear Sunny moving around in the distance. I couldn't imagine what she'd found that had distracted her to the degree she'd apparently ignored me. "What do you have there?" I asked when I noticed she had something in her mouth. She dropped her prize at my feet. I felt my stomach lurch when I saw what she'd been carrying was a shoe. A bloody shoe.

I picked up the bright green tennis shoe and looked around. I didn't see anyone, but the blood on the shoe seemed fresh. "Hey, guys," I called to Mac and Trevor. "I think you'd better come over here."

"Did you find Sunny?" Mac called from across the river.

"I did. But I found something else as well. Something I think you both should see."

"On our way," Mac called.

I returned my attention to the forest surrounding me. It was then I spotted a movement behind the trees. I told Sunny to stay before walking slowly to where it seemed the movement had come from. "Is someone there?" I called out. I waited, but there was no reply. Remembering the bloody shoe, I continued with caution. "Are you in trouble? Do you need help?"

Again, I waited. After a moment I saw an object, or I suppose I should say a person, appear. "I won't hurt you," I said to the apparition.

"You can see me?" asked the ghost, who appeared to be a woman in her late teens or early twenties when alive.

"I can. My name is Amanda. Amanda Parker. What's your name?"

The image before me began to flutter and fade.

"I won't hurt you. I think I can help." I held up the shoe. "Did this belong to you?"

The vision became clearer. "I'm not sure."

I had the distinct feeling the ghost I was speaking to had died recently. Very recently.

"Everything feels so strange," the ghost said.

Mac and Trevor had walked up behind me. I motioned for them to stay back. "I suppose that's understandable."

"Am I dead?"

My heart filled with sympathy. "Yes. It appears you are."

The woman looked at her arm, which was defined but translucent. "I see. Do you know what happened to me?"

"No, I don't. But I can help you find out."

"How?"

"First, why don't you tell me your name and we can figure it out from there?"

The woman frowned. "I'm not sure." She looked around with an expression that reminded me of a frightened deer's. "I can't remember."

"Okay," I said in a soft voice. "That's okay. It isn't uncommon for spirits to become disoriented when they're first separated from their bodies. Maybe we should start by finding your body. Do you remember where you left it?"

The woman faded away. I decided to wait. My sense was that she wanted to find her answers and just needed a moment to gather her thoughts. Eventually, the image returned. Once again, I asked her to lead me to the place where she'd left her body.

"Everything is so fuzzy," she said. "I can't remember who I am or how I got here."

"Okay," I reassured her. "Don't fade away." I gestured behind me. "These are my friends, Mac and Trevor. They'll help me look for your body. I have a feeling it's close by. Is that all right with you?"

She looked as if she might flee, but then nodded. I turned and looked at Mac and Trevor. "I've made contact with a spirit. I would estimate she was in her late teens or early twenties when she passed, and I'm fairly certain that happened recently. She can't remember her name or where her body is, so we're going to help her look for it." I held up the bloody shoe. "I believe this belonged to her. Sunny had it in her mouth when I found her, so I expect the body is close by."

"What do you want us to do?" Trevor asked.

"I want the two of you to take Tucker and continue upstream. I'm going to take Sunny and head off into the woods in the direction I first saw the image appear. Yell if you find anything and I'll do the same. If you don't find anything within a half mile, turn around and come back here."

I called to Sunny and set off into the woods. The ghost seemed content to float along with me. She looked so young. It broke my heart that she most likely had come to a violent end. "Can you remember anything at all yet?" I asked as we walked.

She fluttered in and out but stayed with me. I could sense her confusion. "No." The ghost paused and looked around. "Everything is out of focus."

"Maybe we should start by your telling me anything you do remember."

She took another moment before she began to speak slowly. "I remember seeing the dog with the shoe. I wondered if it was my shoe, and where she'd gotten it. I was trying to remember where I was and how I got here when you called for the dog. I waited for you in the hope you'd be able to help me."

I glanced at Sunny, who was patiently waiting for us to continue our walk. "I don't know what happened to you yet, but I'll help you find out."

"It doesn't seem right that I'm here."

"Why is that?" I asked as I started walking once again, picking my way through the forest as I made my way deeper into the brush.

"I don't know exactly. It just feels wrong. I don't think I've been here before. Nothing is familiar."

"You might just be feeling displaced because of the recent trauma." I looked down at Sunny. She hadn't been trained in search and rescue, but we did play hide and seek. I held the bloody tennis shoe up to her nose. "Find the other one, Sunny. Find the shoe."

Sunny began wagging her whole body. She must think we were going to play a game. She took off running in the opposite direction from which I'd been walking. I didn't have a better idea, so I followed. It didn't take long for her to find a spot in the woods where the ground had recently been disturbed. Sunny started to dig, but I called her away and told her to stay.

"I found something," I called as loudly as I could, hoping Mac and Trevor would hear me. A few breaths later, I heard them call back that they were on their way.

"Is that it?" the woman asked. "Is that where I'm buried?"

"I think so," I answered. "We won't know for sure until we dig. I'm not sure you should be here for this."

"I don't want to be alone."

I found myself wishing Alyson were here, and suddenly she was. I hadn't seen her in over two months and had thought she was gone for good. I was happy to see she wasn't. Alyson was my alter ego who I'd first discovered on returning to Cutter's Cove this summer. I'd learned she was the part of me I'd left behind when I'd returned to New York ten years ago. Initially, she'd existed as an apparition I could see and talk to, but when I decided to stay in Cutter's

Cove, the two of us had become integrated, and most of the time she existed on the inside. She had a way of showing up when I needed her most, however.

"I'll wait with you," Alyson said to the ghost, taking her hand.

"Are you dead too?" the ghost asked.

"No. It's a long story. Come with me and I'll tell you about it."

"Don't go far," I cautioned as Alyson and the ghost disappeared from sight.

I walked toward what I was sure was the shallow grave of a murder victim. There was a trail of blood leading to it. If I had to guess, I'd say the girl had been injured while being pursued by her killer. My chest clenched as my heart broke for someone whose life had been stolen from her much too soon.

"Oh no," Mac said when she arrived and noticed the mound of dirt.

"It looks like you found your ghost's body," Trevor said. He looked around. "Is she still here?"

"Alyson took her somewhere. I'm sure they're nearby. Should we dig ourselves or call Woody?"

"I'd call Woody and wait for him," Mac said.

I held up my phone. "No bars."

"I have a satellite phone," Mac said and took it out. "I'll walk back to that meadow we passed; I should have reception there. I'll have Woody take the waterfall trail and meet us at the foot of the bridge. We can wait for him there and lead him to this spot."

"Yeah, okay. That's a good idea."

"There sure is a lot of blood," Trevor said as we headed to the meadow.

"Yeah." I sighed. "I have a feeling she met with a very violent end."

"Can she remember anything?" Mac asked as we made our way back through the forest.

"She doesn't remember anything that happened before she found herself in the woods watching Sunny with her bloody shoe," I answered. "If her death was as traumatic as it appears, she might be repressing it."

"From the damage to the foliage back there, she must have been chased or pursued," Trevor said.

"I had the same thought," I agreed. "Woody should have some idea."

By the time he arrived with two officers and the body had been dug up, bagged, and taken away, the sun had set and it was close to dark. The area had been sectioned off with crime scene tape and two men in plain clothes had shown up to gather samples and look for physical evidence. The young woman had definitely died from a gunshot wound to the back, and based on the cuts and abrasions on her arms, legs, and feet, it looked as if she'd run through the forest beforehand.

"Any idea who she is?" Woody asked after he'd finished speaking to the men who'd recently arrived.

I shook my head. "She couldn't remember."

"She *couldn't remember*?"

"The woman who was killed. The reason I even knew to look for the body in the first place was because I stumbled across her ghost. Unfortunately, when I asked her who she was, she couldn't remember. I think she has amnesia."

"Amnesia?" Woody looked doubtful but eventually shrugged. "Okay. The crime scene guys are going to take over now. I'm heading back to the office. I'll see if I can figure out who the victim is. I'll call you once I get an ID."

"Thanks. And thanks for responding so quickly."

"It's my job," he reminded me.

Of course it was his job to recover the bodies of murder victims, but it wasn't his job to suspend disbelief when fed a story about amnesiac ghosts, but he did it anyway. When he left and the crime scene guys moved on to check out the perimeter, I called to Alyson. She reappeared, along with the woman whose body had just been found.

"What happened?" she asked.

"You were shot and buried here, but it appears you ran through the woods before that, I imagine to escape your killer. Do you have any idea at all where you were prior to being here?"

She shook her head, looking interested but not overly traumatized. I had a feeling she hadn't quite made the connection between her current state and the body that had just been taken away. "Do you know who I am?"

"Not yet, but we'll find out. It's important that you move on to the next life now that your spirit has departed. I think Alyson can help you do that."

She shook her head. "Not until I know. I don't remember who I was, but I have to assume there are people who cared about me. I need to be sure they get the answers they need. Once I'm certain they're okay, I can move on."

I glanced at Alyson, who shrugged. "Okay," I said. "I suggest you come home with us until we have your answers. Alyson can show you the way. Is that all right with you?"

She nodded. "Yes."

Alyson and the woman disappeared. I wasn't sure how either Alyson or the ghosts I had come into contact with moved through time and space; they seemed to be where they wanted or needed to be.

"Let's go," I said to Mac and Trevor. "Alyson is taking her to the house."

"I'm kind of surprised she showed up again," Trevor said. "Didn't you think she was gone for good?"

I shrugged. "I have no idea how it works. I haven't seen her for two months but today, when I needed her, she was willing and able to help."

"You can ask Chan about it," Mac suggested, referring to our friend, who owned a magic shop and seemed to be a lot better versed in all things supernatural than I.

"I will. It'd be nice to know I can count on her when I need her."

It was completely dark by the time we hiked out of the forest and returned to the house. I fed both dogs, then went in search of my cat, Shadow, who, interestingly enough, could see both Alyson and the ghosts who came into my life. His ability has helped me on more than one occasion.

Trevor offered to start dinner while I went upstairs to try to connect with Alyson and the ghost. If Woody didn't come up with a name pretty quickly, we'd need to assign her a temporary one. Continuing to call her *the ghost* would become awkward. Mac had gone up to her office to check her emails and to call Ty Matthews, the man she was romantically interested in, though she'd only admit to him being her business partner. I figured I had at least twenty minutes of quiet time.

"Alyson, are you here?" I called.

After a moment, she appeared.

"Is our ghost friend with you?"

"She is." Alyson looked to her side. "You can appear. It's safe here."

"Did you find out who I am?" she asked.

"Not yet. But we're working on it. In the meantime, are you okay with Alyson?"

She nodded.

"Is there a name we can use to refer to you? Something temporary, until you learn your real name?"

"Anything is fine."

I glanced at her. "Is there a name that comes to you? One tickling the corner of your mind?"

"Sissy. I think I was called Sissy, although I don't think it was my name."

"Sissy is a good name. That's what we'll call you until you remember your real name. I don't expect to hear from the police for a while yet. I'm not sure how time and space work exactly where you are, but feel free to hang around here. I'll make sure you know it when I have news to share."

"Okay. And thank you. It will be nice to remember."

As Alyson and Sissy faded away, I headed downstairs to join Trevor in the kitchen. My mom had gone back to New York for a few months but had plans to return to Cutter's Cove for Christmas. Mac and I had settled into a routine of either picking up takeout or making something simple for dinner on most nights, but when Trevor wasn't working, he usually cooked for us. Sometimes we dined at his home on the beach, other times he did the honors in my kitchen, but wherever the food was made, you could bet it was going to be wonderful.

"Smells like garlic," I said to my tall, dark-haired friend as I poured myself a glass of wine and sat down at the kitchen counter.

Trevor shot me a half grin. "I'm making a seafood chowder with the shrimp, crab, and scallops I found in your freezer. It's quick and hearty, with potatoes and carrots and seafood simmered in a lemon garlic broth. Do you have any bread we can heat up? This is the sort of dish you'll want to eat with bread for dipping."

"I have several loaves of heat-and-serve bread in the freezer. Not as good as fresh, but pretty good in a pinch. Mac and I don't cook a lot, so I haven't been keeping fresh ingredients on hand. Maybe we can go into town tomorrow to pick up some fresh seafood and greens from the farmers market, and bread from the bakery."

"That sounds great." Trevor tasted the broth, then added several spices from my mother's rack. "Have you heard from Woody? We talked about heading to Dooley's Farm tomorrow to pick up the pumpkins for the decorations for the fund-raiser, but I wasn't sure how the arrival of the newest ghost in your life might impact that."

"I haven't heard from him. If I don't by the time we finish eating dinner, I'll call him. Unless there's a missing persons report or some other readily available way to identify her, it might not be all that easy."

Trevor turned the heat down and covered the pot. "Someone must be missing her."

"I agree. Sissy seems to be very concerned with finding out who she is so she can make sure the people she might have left behind know what happened to her."

"She remembered her name?"

"No. Sissy is a temporary name. I figured if she didn't remember her real name soon, we'd be stuck calling her *the ghost* for who knows how long." I got up and crossed the room to click on the gas fire in the fireplace built into the back wall of the kitchen. When Mom and I bought the house, the fireplace had used logs, but when we remodeled we switched to gas. The only fireplace in the house that still used real wood was the one in the living room.

"I've been thinking it might be fun to convert that fireplace into a brick pizza oven. It wouldn't be all that difficult to do, and you've been looking for ways to make the space yours," Trevor suggested.

"I love the idea, but I don't know how to make pizza. If I do convert it, you'll have to come over and make use of it."

"Seems like I'm over here every night I'm not working anyway. The oven could still be used as an accent piece even when you weren't making pizza. We'd create a large arched opening here." Trevor outlined the area with his hand. "The flames inside the oven would be visible from the seating area and could be turned on whether you were cooking or not. In fact, I've seen brick pizza ovens with a larger opening lower in the brick for a regular fireplace, then a smaller opening for the pizza oven above that. I can draw you a design if you're interested."

"Yeah, do it. It sounds like a lovely idea. I've been thinking about building a wine cellar in the basement, or at least part of the basement. Between that and the pizza oven, the house will take on an old-world Italian feel. At least this part of the house anyway. I'm not sure why, but that appeals to me."

Trevor placed the bread on a cookie sheet and popped it in the oven. "I love the idea of a wine cellar. The space isn't being used right now, so you may as well add some charm and functionality to it. I can build you wine racks when you're ready. I have some repurposed wood that would work really well."

"Sounds awesome. It'd be fun to go wine tasting and select some bottles once we finish the space."

"There are a ton of really great wineries in the Willamette Valley. I went with a group a few years ago. We made a weekend of it and had the best time. Maybe the three of us could work out a tour. There are some really nice bed-and-breakfasts in the area."

"Sounds like fun."

"This will be ready in about fifteen minutes. I'll run up to let Mac know. The soup is on simmer, so it should be fine until I get back, but you might want to keep your eye on the bread."

I took a peek at the bread, which looked to have at least another fifteen minutes, then wandered onto the deck. It was a cold but clear night, with just a hint of a breeze. The sound of the waves crashing onto the rocks below was somewhat muted, indicating to me that the tide was most likely low. I'd stood out on this deck listening to the waves and looking at the stars overhead hundreds of times before. I was happiest and most at home on this deck, but tonight I felt a lingering sadness as I thought about Sissy and the life that had been taken from her much too soon. I couldn't imagine what had happened to her. Given the number of scrapes and abrasions on her body, it looked as if she'd run heedlessly through the forest for quite some time before being gunned down.

"It's dark." Alyson suddenly appeared next to me.

"Yes. I can see that."

"No, I don't mean the sky. It's Sissy. Her mind is dark."

I frowned. "You can see into her mind?"

"Not really." Alyson frowned. "Well, sort of. It's hard to explain."

"Can you see what happened to her?" I asked.

"I can't tell you what happened to her, but I can tell you that any memories she's had have been wiped clean. It's as if she never even existed before today."

Okay, that was strange. At least I thought it was strange. I was no expert on either amnesia or ghosts, but I guess I assumed her memories were there but inaccessible. "Maybe her memories will come back with time. I'm going to do everything I can to help her find her answers. It must be so strange not to remember anything from her life."

"I'm sure she finds it unsettling."

I smiled at Alyson. "I'm glad you're here. I've missed you."

"I'm always here with you, only on the inside. I'm looking forward to the fund-raiser. We'll need a new dress."

"The masquerade ball is going to be a big deal. If things go as planned, Caleb is hoping to raise enough money to expand the children's wing at the hospital."

Caleb Wellington, along with his fiancée, Chelsea Green, had set up a charitable foundation with part of the money he'd inherited from his grandfather, Barkley Cutter. Both Caleb and Chelsea had grown up in Cutter's Cove and had deep ties to the place. It was here, they'd decided, they'd share their wealth and raise a family. The idea for the masquerade ball was Chelsea's, but once Caleb had latched onto it, he'd made it his own by incorporating the props he'd developed over the years working on the annual Halloween Haunted Hayride. The ball was set to take place in the house philanthropist Booker Oswald had donated to the historical society. In addition to providing an elegant affair, Caleb planned to create an enchanted environment similar to that of a haunted mansion. I thought the event was going to be spectacular.

"I was thinking a simple but elegant long black dress with a black sequined mask," Alyson continued. "We might even want to consider a long black wig to give our costume the Morticia Addams feel. Not that people are necessarily dressing up, but I think a wig would be fun."

I chuckled. "Do you know how odd it is for me to be having a conversation with myself?"

Alyson smiled and shrugged. "Stranger things have happened to us."

"I guess that's true. I'm not sure about the wig, but a long black dress sounds great. We'll go shopping this week."

"Tomorrow?"

"No. Not tomorrow," I answered. "I'm hoping to work on Sissy's murder case, and we're supposed to help Chelsea decorate tomorrow. The ball isn't until Saturday, so we'll have plenty of time to run over to Portland and look for a dress." I glanced at the door. "I think Trev has dinner ready. Keep an eye on Sissy and let me know if she begins to remember."

"I will, but I don't think she will. At least not without help."

"Then we'll find a way to help her. Maybe Mac can run her image though her facial recognition program if Woody can give us a photo. It's a long shot, but it might turn something up. In the meantime, there's a bowl of seafood chowder and a glass of wine with my name on it."

I turned around to go back inside when a chill ran down my spine. I looked around but didn't see anything out of place. Still I had one of those distinct feelings you get when you're being watched. I could see the ocean in the distance and the wide-open feel of the meadow leading up to the edge of the bluff. Both appeared to be empty. It was dark, so I couldn't see anything beyond the tree line in the distance, but I doubted anyone was there. I might just be spooked after what had happened today. After all, a young woman was dead, and as far as I knew, her killer was still out there.

Chapter 2

Monday, October 22

I'm not sure what prompted me to wake up in the middle of the night and look at my cell phone. I'm not usually one of those people who checks her phone for messages around the clock. Still, when I awoke at two a.m. I picked up my cell and clicked on the Home screen. "Oh God," I said aloud, a simple yet alarming communication appearing before me.

I sat up and turned on the light. Both Tucker and Sunny looked at me oddly as I gripped the phone in my hand and stared at the screen, which revealed a photo with nine little words written beneath it: *She who spills the blood must pay the price.*

The photo was an old image of Mario and Clay Bonatello that had to have been taken at least fifteen years before. Maybe longer. Mario and Clay were part of a known Mafia family and the reason Mom and I went into witness protection and moved to Cutter's Cove when I was a teenager. The brothers had been dead for more than ten years. It made no sense that anyone would be sending me a photo of them now. And yet the evidence in my hand proved someone had done just that.

My nightmare had begun on a sunny spring day more than thirteen years ago. My best friend Tiffany and I had cut school to go to the beach. But Tiffany had arranged for a ride from some guy she'd met in a club, and instead of heading in the right direction, we'd ended up being dumped in a bad part of the city just in time to see Mario and Clay kill a man gangland style. I'd tried to hide, in the hope they wouldn't spot us, but Tiffany had screamed, and suddenly, they were after us. The next thing I knew, I was taken into custody by federal marshals who told me Tiffany was dead and I was the only witness to what turned out to be a very important murder. Mario and Clay had gone underground, and it was decided I needed to disappear until they could be found and arrested. It was a difficult time in my life, but I was warned it was my best option if I didn't want to end up sharing Tiffany's fate. Mom had agreed to go with me, so my handler, Donovan, killed off Amanda and Estelle Parker in a fiery car wreck and Alyson and Sarah Prescott were born.

While Amanda and Estelle had lived the life of wealthy New Yorkers, Alyson and Sarah were relocated to a small town on the Oregon coast, where we settled down in the heart of the middle class. Despite the circumstances, we'd actually been quite happy in Cutter's Cove. Sure, there were things we missed, especially the people we'd left behind, but we made new friends and had what we both considered a good life.

Then, two years later, Clay and Mario found out where I was, and my life was once again in danger. It looked as if we'd need to run yet again when we got a message from Donovan that the elders in the Bonatello family had decided they were tired of cleaning up the brothers' messes and they were eliminated by their own people. Suddenly, Mom and I could come out of hiding. We left Cutter's Cove and returned to New York.

I had no idea who had sent the photo to my phone. Clay and Mario were long dead, and I didn't think it was widely known what had happened to them outside the Bonatello family. I'd been assured that the rest of the family had no beef with me, so it didn't make sense that the people who had killed them would now be after me. I wasn't sure what was going on, but I did know what I needed to do next. As soon as it was late enough, I called Donovan.

"Amanda," Donovan said. "It's been a while since we've spoken."

"Not since I graduated college. How's everything been with you?"

"Fine, but I have a feeling you haven't called to chat after all this time."

"I didn't." Then I told him about the message.

My words were met with silence and then a sigh. "I was afraid of something like this."

"You were? Why? I thought I was in the clear. I thought the family decided I wasn't a threat to them. I thought they'd assured you that they would leave me alone."

"All of that was true, but there have been some developments."

"Developments? What kind of developments?"

"Five top-ranking members of the Bonatello family have been murdered in the last three months, including Franco Bonatello, the highest of all. So far, no arrests have been made, but the feds suspect Vito Bonatello might be behind all five murders."

"Who's Vito Bonatello?"

"Clay's son. He was in prison when his father shot the man in the Manhattan parking lot and then went after Tiffany. He just got out six months ago. Three months later, Franco was found dead. Since then, four other family members have been shot to death, and Vito is now the head of the Bonatello family."

"So you think he knows his father was killed by the family for pursuing me and is now out for my blood?"

"I think it's a possibility. Maybe I should bring you in."

"No," I said. "I'm not going that route again. I'll keep my eyes open and my head down, but I'm not giving up my life again."

Donovan sighed. "Okay. It's your choice. As far as I can tell, Vito is in New York, trying to solidify his position in the family, which I can assure you is far from secure. I don't necessarily suspect you're in any immediate danger. He may not even know you've left the city. Was the message sent to your New York cell number?"

"It was. I haven't gotten around to changing it. I'm not even sure I will."

"Don't. At least not for now. If Vito thinks you're in New York, let him. In the meantime, I'll see what I can find out. Forward the message to me and I'll have a team do some digging."

"Okay. And thanks. I'm sorry to have to bother you. I imagine you thought you were through with me."

Donovan chuckled. "While I'm not happy about the message you received, I'm happy to have had a reason for us to catch up. I've missed you."

"I've missed you too. Did your brother ever get married? The last time we spoke, he was engaged but had been suffering from a severe case of cold feet."

"He did get married and has twin daughters. However, I do have an interesting story. Remember my …"

Donovan and I spent the next twenty minutes catching up with each other. I really had missed him. We'd been close when my life was in danger, and by the end of my time in witness protection, I'd considered him an honorary uncle of sorts. I couldn't begin to describe the bond that can be forged when your life is literally in the hands of someone whose job it is to make sure you're protected from some very bad people.

After I hung up the phone I decided to go about my normal routine, which, since coming back to Cutter's Cove, consisted of taking Sunny and Tucker out for a walk as soon as I woke up. I had every reason to obsess over the text, but experience had shown me that that had never gotten me anywhere. I was going to ignore the text and pick up my day where it had left off. The waking-up-early part was already taken care of because I'd never gotten back to sleep after receiving the photo, so the walk was the next item on my agenda. Tucker was twelve years old and liked to lumber along at a much slower pace than Sunny, who I estimated to be between one and two, so we'd settled into a pattern in which I'd walk slow enough for Tucker to follow comfortably, while Sunny ran ahead and then back to us, then back ahead again, tripling, at least, the distance she traveled. Once we made our way to the bluff overlooking the rough sea, Tucker and I would sit for a while, enjoying the spectacular view, before heading back home for coffee and conversation with Mac on the deck at the back of the house.

Despite my resolve, I found I was having a hard time focusing on the day ahead rather than on the photo, but I wasn't going to let an ex-con bully ruin my life again. I had a ghost with amnesia to worry about, and that was where I was determined to direct my attention, unless Donovan got back to me with news that would justify immediate action on my part.

When Sunny had had her share of exercise for the morning, the dogs and I headed back to the house.

"It's going to be cool today," Mac, who was wrapped up in a blanket sipping coffee from a lounge chair, commented.

"I think the high temperature is only supposed to be around sixty. It'll be nice to have crisp weather for tromping around the pumpkin patch."

Mac cradled her mug with both hands before taking another sip of hot liquid. "Trevor and I went to Dooley's Farm every fall when we were growing up. And then you'd come with us when you lived in Cutter's Cove. I haven't been there once since senior year of high school. First I was in college and then I was living in California. I'm really looking forward to going back today."

"Did Trev say what time he'd be by to pick us up?" I asked.

"He said around ten. He wanted to make sure he'd completed his payroll and some other accounting chores beforehand."

"That's just as well." I stretched out my legs in front of me and rested my feet on the railing that offered protection from the rocky shoreline below. "I have some images I need to upload and send off, and Mom wanted me to pick out some of my better photos to be framed and matted for the gallery. I could use a couple of hours at the computer."

"Have you heard from Woody?" Mac wondered.

"No. I suppose I should call him. Alyson seems to think Sissy's memories have been wiped clean, but that doesn't seem right to me. I can buy that she might not have access to them right now, but they must still be hanging around somewhere in her mind."

"Maybe she was dropped here from the future and before she was sent back in time someone used one of those *Men in Black* devices on her." Mac grinned.

I smiled back. "I sort of doubt it."

"Maybe she's a robot."

"Robots aren't human; they can't die or become ghosts."

Mac chuckled. "Good point. Hopefully, Woody will have run her prints and know who she is by now."

"If he hasn't identified her, I wonder if you could run her image through your facial recognition software. Providing Woody can supply a photo of her, of course."

"I would need my desktop computer for that, and I haven't set it up yet because I'll need to upgrade the electrical system going into that room. I can ask Ty to run it with his equipment, though. He has a lot better equipment than I do anyway."

"Okay, great. I'll let you know what Woody says when I have a chance to speak to him."

When I called Woody a bit later, I learned he'd run her prints, but they weren't in the system. He'd also done an extensive search for a missing persons report that matched Sissy's description but had come up empty. It didn't seem right to either of us that there wasn't anyone out there looking for her. I asked him about a photo and he said the body had been taken to the county morgue, but he'd see what he could do. Other than that, he promised to keep me in the loop.

I took a shower and dressed for a day at the pumpkin patch. I still had some time until Trevor planned to pick us up, and I spent it going through all my photos, trying to figure out which I'd set aside for the magazine, which I'd put on my website to sell as stock photos, and which I'd sharpen and polish for Mom to sell at her gallery. I was really enjoying my new career as a freelance graphic artist and photographer. I didn't need the money I earned from the images I produced, so the pressure was off to sell more than I had time to capture and process. But the endeavor gave me a creative outlet I was finding I rather enjoyed. Between the photography, the work I was doing on the house, and the ghost hunting, I had a lot to occupy my mind and my time.

******

"Chelsea wants a lot of pumpkins," Mac informed us. "She's not only going to decorate the entry, she wants pumpkins to use in the yard as accents to the fall flowers and shrubs Booker planted."

"Let's each get a wagon. That'll save us time," I suggested. "We can purchase and load each wagonful into Trevor's truck as we find the best ones."

"Is she only looking for large pumpkins?" Trevor asked.

"She wants large pumpkins to use as accent pieces in the yard, but a variety of sizes for the foyer," Mac answered. "She also mentioned wanting some smaller pumpkins as well as leaves and a mix of smaller gourds to use for the tables in the dining area."

We each grabbed one of the wagons the farm provided and headed through the forest toward the patch of flat ground where the pumpkins grew. Dooley's sold apples and pumpkins in the fall, Christmas trees in December, and berries and seasonal produce in the spring and early summer. In addition to the fruits, vegetables, and trees they sold, they offered hay rides and an indoor/outdoor restaurant that served burgers, sandwiches, and seasonal specialties.

"Even though the wagons are a good size, we're going to have to make a lot of trips to the truck to get all the pumpkins Chelsea wants," Trevor commented.

I shrugged. "That's fine. It's a nice day and we're getting a good workout. Maybe we can stop to take a break partway through. I've been dreaming of Dooley's pumpkin ice cream."

"Oh, and their apple pie with cinnamon sauce," Mac added. "I've missed that pie." She looked at Trevor. "Amanda and I were discussing how long it had been since we'd been here. Did you come out every year after we left town?"

"Not every year, but I came a few times. I dated a woman two Halloweens ago who had two children from a previous marriage. They were five and seven then, and we had a fantastic time picking out pumpkins and eating junk food."

"Are you talking about the real estate agent who decided to move back to Maryland to be close to her parents?" Mac asked.

Trevor nodded. "Yes, that was the one."

"I remember her leaving was tough on you," Mac said.

"It was, at the time. But we keep in touch, and she's very happy with her decision. She's engaged now, to a guy she dated in high school, and she assures me he's a great guy who'll be a good father to the kids. I'm happy for all of them."

I wasn't sure why exactly, but somehow a discussion revolving around Trevor's dating life put a damper on the perfection of the day, at least for me, so I changed the subject. "So, the charity ball is on Saturday, but what about Halloween? Should we plan something?" I looked at Trevor. "Are you going to be open?"

"Pirates Pizza will be open. The town is doing a trick-or-treat thing; it has for the past several years. All the merchants on Main Street stay open until nine. We decorate and hand out candy. I plan to offer some specialty pizzas with a Halloween theme. I'd love it if you would both come by to help out. There's usually a big turnout, so I could use help handing out candy and seating the customers who want to stay for a bite to eat."

"I'm in," I said.

"Yeah, me too," Mac added. "It sounds like fun. Should we dress up?"

"A costume is optional, but most of the merchants make the effort. If you do dress up, bring something to change into and we can go out after. There are a couple of bars in town that are planning to have live music and drink specials."

It took us almost an hour to fill half the bed of Trevor's truck. We decided to take a break and grab something to eat before starting on the second half. We weren't sure exactly how many pumpkins Chelsea wanted, but she'd told Mac she wanted a lot, so that was what we were going to bring her. It was fun gathering the pumpkins, and I figured they could be my donation to the cause.

We were just finishing our burgers when I got a call from Woody. "Did you find something?" I asked.

"We still don't have an identity, but the medical examiner sent over his initial report. Jane Doe was shot in the back by a high-powered rifle. The sort one might use to hunt big game."

"So you think she was shot by a hunter? Could it have been an accident?"

"Unlikely. From all the cuts and bruises on her torso, I'd wager she ran through the forest for quite some time before she was shot. The burial site appears to be the actual place she died, although we found a trail of blood indicating she'd been bleeding for a while before she was shot."

"So her killer pursued her." I voiced the thought I'd had when I'd first found the body.

"Yes, it looks that way. We found the shoe matching the one Sunny had in her mouth in the woods not far away. I'm having the lab test it for DNA."

"Do you think it's odd that no one has reported her missing?" I asked.

"Not necessarily. She might live alone, or maybe she was traveling through the area and no one realizes she's missing yet. It might take some time, but we'll figure out who she was. Unless something more urgent comes up, I plan to commit all my time to it today."

"We're gathering pumpkins for Chelsea Green to use as decorations for Saturday's ball today, but if you stumble onto anything you want us to follow up on, please call. I'd like to help my ghost friend move on as soon as possible."

"Will do. Have fun at the pumpkin patch."

I filled Mac and Trevor in on my conversation with Woody, then we headed back out to gather the rest of the pumpkins we planned to donate to the charity ball. It took two more hours to completely fill the truck, but once it was up to capacity, we drove to the oceanfront mansion where the ball was to be held. Booker's niece, Monica, who lived in the house and acted as its caretaker, was in the front garden with Chelsea when we arrived. The place looked spectacular. Chelsea had brought in bales of hay that had been decoratively stacked. There were tall corn stalks on the wide front porch and huge planters overflowing with fall flowers that accented the trees and shrubs Booker had planted. Caleb had hooked up some of his mechanical monsters, which were strategically placed to add interest but not to be overwhelming. Once the pumpkins we'd brought had been set up too, the grounds were going to look magical.

"Wow, this place looks awesome," I said as we climbed out of the truck.

"It really is coming together nicely," Chelsea agreed. "Thanks for getting the pumpkins. It would have taken me all day."

"We were happy to make the trip," I answered. "Where do you want them?"

"I want the largest ones for the grounds. Maybe just set them near the hay bales or in the garden. I'd like some large- to mid-size pumpkins for the porch as well. We can take the others inside for the entry display and the tables. I thought about decorating the ballroom, but I think it's going to be pretty crowded as it is."

"Ticket sales are good?" Mac asked.

Chelsea nodded. "We sold out a couple of days ago. I have two tickets for each of you, as requested."

"Do you need some money?" Trevor asked.

"Amanda had me charge them to her credit card. You can square things up with her."

"So, does the fact that you sold out mean you met your fund-raising goal?" Trevor asked.

"No. Not by a long shot. The real money is going to come from the silent auction. I've managed to gather an awesome selection of items I hope will bring in the money we need. I just hope everyone comes with their checkbooks. I know most folks realize how important the children's wing at the hospital is to the community, so I'm anticipating some strong bids." Chelsea looked at me. "I wish I'd have thought to talk to your mother about a painting when she was here. A signed Estelle Parker would have brought in a lot of money."

"Actually, there are some signed paintings at the house. I'm sure she'd like to donate one. I'll call her to talk about it."

Chelsea smiled. "That would be great. I still can't believe the woman I knew for two years as your very cool but totally average mother was *the* Estelle Parker."

******

After we got home I called Donovan. As hard as I'd tried, I couldn't get the text I'd received out of my mind. "I know we just spoke this morning, but have you heard anything?" I asked when he picked up.

"I've confirmed Vito Bonatello is here in New York. I can't be sure he's the one who sent the message to you, but I still suspect he was. My sources tell me that with the power structure in the family severely damaged and threats coming in from other families, Vito has his hands full at the moment and most likely won't be leaving the city any time soon."

"Do you think he might send someone after me?"

Donovan paused. "I don't think so, but Vito has an agenda of his own I know nothing about. If you're at all worried, I can bring you in."

"No. I just want to know what's going on so I can be prepared."

"With the degree of pressure he must be feeling from all sides, I don't think he'd spare any of his muscle to come after you right now. And as we said, because the message was sent to your New York City cell number, the odds are that Vito, or whoever sent the message for him, believes you're still in New York. I'll keep my ear to the ground to see if I can pick up any chatter. I have an informant in the family who hasn't heard your name mentioned, but she'll let me know if she does."

"Is your informant close to Vito?"

"A cousin. She isn't part of Vito's inner circle, but she's a good listener and picks up on things. Of course, she swears she had no idea Vito planned to kill five members of the family."

"Are you sure he's the one who killed them?"

"Actually, no. He's the one who seemed to have the most motive for wanting the first victim dead, however. Franco was the one who gave the order to have his father killed. The fact that Franco's death coincided with Vito's release from prison makes him an even better suspect. Add to that the fact that he's now the one in power and it's hard to argue against him as the killer. Still, as far as I know, we don't have anything that even remotely resembles proof."

"Lack of proof is the way the families operate, isn't it, so I guess I shouldn't be surprised."

"True. I'll call you tomorrow to check in with you. And if you get any more messages or sense you're in any danger, call me anytime, day or night."

"Okay. Thanks, Donovan. I'll keep my eyes open, but I'll try not to worry."

******

Later that evening, Mac, Trevor, and I gathered all the animals and headed over to Trevor's place. I hadn't heard from Alyson since the day before, but I figured she was around somewhere. I assumed if Sissy had moved on, Alyson would find a way to tell me. The fact that neither had put in an appearance when we arrived home from our day at the pumpkin patch didn't have me worried. Exactly.

Although it was a cool evening, we decided to share a bottle of wine on the deck. Trevor built a fire in the pit and we all wore jackets, making an evening of enjoying the waves rolling onto the deserted beach enjoyable. Trevor had a casserole in the oven. He hadn't said what kind, but it smelled heavenly. I was still getting used to the idea that my goofy friend from high school had grown up to be someone who both owned a business and could cook.

"Before you leave this evening, I want to show you the table I'm working on for your entry," Trevor said.

"You're working on a table for my entry?" I asked.

"I found a huge piece of driftwood after the big storm we had at the end of August. It had a beautiful grain and texture and I wanted to do something special with it. You don't have to put it in your entry if you decide the table isn't to your taste or you're going for a different look, but when I got the wood shaped and sanded down, I thought it would be perfect for your house. I can stain it any color you want, but I'm thinking of something dark to give it a rich, Old World feel."

"It sounds fantastic." I smiled. "I'm anxious to take a look at it."

"I want a Trevor Johnson original for my room," Mac said.

"And I'd love for you to have one. What are you thinking? A table? Dresser? Desk?"

Mac paused, I assumed to consider the question. "I'm not sure. I was thinking of a table because we've just been talking about tables, but a desk would be awesome. I'd want something that looked rustic and natural, but I'd also like it to be functional. Drawers that glide easily, as well as a place for cords and maybe even a USB port."

"Seems doable. The next time I'm at the house we can take a look at the size and shape that would work best. I'll have more time to work in the shop over the winter, when the days are short and I won't be out surfing as much."

"I bet the view is pretty awesome when winter storms roll in," I said.

"It is. You'll have to come over and storm watch with me sometime. It's really spectacular when it snows."

"I bet it is."

"I need to head inside to check on my casserole," Trevor informed us. "More wine?"

Mac and I both indicated we'd like more, but rather than have him bring it to us, we went inside so we could sit in his kitchen to talk to him while he finished making our dinner. I'd just settled in at the large counter when I received a text from Woody.

"Woody just sent me a photo of our mystery ghost." I couldn't help but grimace just a bit; it had been taken after the medical examiner had done his thing. I looked at Mac. "Is Ty willing to try to track her down?"

"He said he'd do what he could. Forward the photo to me and I'll send it on to him."

I did as Mac requested. "Be forewarned: It isn't a pretty picture."

Mac's phone dinged. She looked at the text and frowned. "Got it. I'll call Ty to let him know I'm sending the photo." She stood up. "I'll just go back out to the deck to make the call."

"Dinner will be ready in ten minutes," Trevor said.

"I'll make it quick," Mac promised.

After Mac left I turned my attention to Trevor. It was nice to sit and chat with him while he cooked. I'd never dated anyone who liked to cook, but I had to admit I found it kind of a turn-on. Not that I'd ever tell Trevor that. Not that I should even be thinking that. I needed to think about something else. "It seems a little weird Woody hasn't been able to turn up anything on Sissy," I eventually commented.

"Maybe she isn't from around here," Trevor suggested. "She might have been just passing through when she met up with whoever killed her."

"Woody made a similar comment. I guess if she was from out of town there may not be an easy way to backtrack to figure out who she is."

"She looked to be young. Maybe not even eighteen."

"Yeah." I sighed. "She did look fairly young, but some people have features that make them appear younger than they are. If she wasn't from around here, Woody might be facing a real challenge. It would be a lot easier if Sissy could remember who she was in life."

"Maybe she will. I seem to remember you telling me that other ghosts you've helped in the past started off pretty confused, but small details began to come to them over time."

"That's true. We'll just need to keep working the case until we have the answers we need."

Chapter 3

Friday, October 26

It had been four days since I'd first learned of Vito Bonatello and his presumed campaign to take over the Bonatello family, and five days since we'd found Sissy's body. The good news was that Donovan hadn't picked up any chatter that would suggest I was in any immediate danger, and I hadn't received any additional messages. The bad news was that we were no closer to identifying Sissy than we'd been on day one. Ty had come up blank on the facial recognition search and Woody still hadn't been able to find anyone who'd reported Sissy missing. Additionally, the medical examiner and crime scene guys hadn't found anything specific enough on her body or clothing to provide an actual lead. I hadn't had the opportunity to chat with Sissy since Sunday, but I had connected with Alyson, who'd assured me that Sissy was still around, just depressed, so she preferred to hang out in the void rather than spend time in the land of the living. We talked about it at length and realized it was going to be difficult to convince a depressed ghost to move on if we were unable to identify her, but it hadn't even been a week yet, so it felt much too soon to give up altogether.

Mac and I went to Portland yesterday to buy dresses for the ball. We'd met up with Ty for lunch, and I had to admit Mac knew how to pick 'em. Not only was he supersmart, he was really nice and extremely good-looking. And from the way he hung on Mac's every word, I'd say he was as interested in her as she was in him. I wasn't sure why they were taking so much time to move things along, although their love life was none of my business and I'd vowed to stay out of it. Ty was coming to the charity ball tomorrow evening and planned to spend the night in the guest room on the third floor after the event. I wondered if that was where he'd end up.

Again, none of my business.

Neither Trevor nor I had a romantic interest we planned to bring to the ball, but we did each have an extra ticket we didn't want to waste, so I invited Woody and Trev invited Brooklyn Fenway, a new teacher at the high school this year who Trevor had met while surfing. I hadn't had the opportunity to meet her yet, but Trevor assured me that she was very nice and would fit in well with our group. After a bit of discussion, we decided to hire a limo and the six of us would attend the ball together. I was looking forward to the evening despite the little voice in the back of my mind, that I was certain was Alyson, warning me it might have been better to waste the extra tickets then to encourage Trevor to bring a date.

My plan for today was to take the dogs and my camera and head out into nature to capture what was left of the beautiful fall foliage. The shots I'd taken with my phone on Sunday had turned out fantastic and I wondered what sort of shots I could get with my 35 millimeter, lenses, and filters. I planned to start off along the coast trail, but if I had enough time and the right light, I might head back toward the waterfall as well. Maybe I'd drive out to Dooley's Farm, park in the lot, and begin with photos of people searching the pumpkin patch for the perfect jack-o'-lanterns. Once I had my fill of photos from there and the adjoining corn maze, I'd head up the hill where Farmer Dooley grew the Christmas trees he sold between Thanksgiving and Christmas Eve. If I continued on to the top of the hill, I'd meet up with a narrow trail that wound its way through the national forest. Once I'd gotten the shots I hoped for along this deserted piece of forest, I'd circle back to the parking area.

Figuring my hike would take most of the day, I packed trail mix, fruit, and plenty of water for me and the dogs. I chose two of my more versatile lenses, a few filters I felt might come in handy, and my Nikon and set out on my grand adventure.

As predicted, the pumpkin patch netted me a plethora of colorful seasonal images, and the walk through the forest resulted in several images I was sure were going to end up being gallery quality. When the dogs and I got to a beautiful fall meadow, I sat down on a log so Tucker could rest. I gave both dogs water, as well as some of my trail mix and a granola bar. I closed my eyes and let the sound of the leaves rustling in the wind lull me into a state of bliss as the soft breeze caressed my face and the tension eased from my body.

It was while I was reveling in nature's beauty that Donovan called, shattering my feeling of contentment. "I have news."

"Good news or bad news?" I asked.

"It depends on how you look at it. First, I need to confirm that the text you received with the photo of the Bonatello brothers came through at some point during the early morning hours on Monday, October 22."

"Yes, that's right. I woke up at around two a.m. and checked my phone. The home page notified me that I had a message. It hadn't been there when I'd gone to bed the night before."

"That's what I thought. I just learned Vito was being held for questioning regarding the family members who've died. He was brought in on the afternoon of the twenty-first and wasn't released until the afternoon of the twenty-second."

"So he couldn't have sent the message I received."

"Exactly. Is there a phone number associated with the message?"

"It just says unknown. I guess whoever sent it used a burner."

"And you haven't received any additional texts?"

"No."

I could hear Donovan let out a breath. "I'm going to have someone from the field office in Portland come by to pick up your phone. He'll bring you a new one with an unlisted number. Will you be around this afternoon?"

"I can be, but I'm hiking right now and it will take me a while to get home. I'll call you when I get there."

"Okay. I'll get the meeting set up."

After I hung up, I took a minute to gather my thoughts. Was I really getting pulled back into the witness protection thing? I supposed the choice was mine to make. For now, I'd try not to panic. I did, however, feel I should tell Mac and Trevor what was going on. Mac was living in the house with me, which could put her in danger if someone knew my current whereabouts. I worried what this would do to my newfound happiness. Would the situation linger over my head for years, as it had the last time? God, I hoped not.

I got up and started to loop back toward where I'd left my car when I heard the voice. "Can you help me? I seem to have lost my way."

I opened my eyes and was surprised to see the person who'd spoken to me wasn't a living person at all but another ghost. "I can help you," I said. "My name is Amanda. What's yours?"

The ghost frowned. "Josie."

"Do you have a last name, Josie?"

"I'm not sure. I've been trying to remember, but everything is fuzzy. Somehow, I got lost in these woods. I've been wandering around for what seems like a very long time, but no matter how far I walk, I can't seem to find my way back to the road."

I stifled a groan as I realized Sissy's murder might not have been an isolated incident. "I'm afraid the reason you can't find the road is because you appear to be trapped in another dimension."

"I'm dead, aren't I?"

I nodded. "I'm afraid so."

"I thought as much, but I didn't want to believe it. I've tried talking to a lot of different people, but you're the only one who's responded. If I'm dead, why can you see me? Are you dead too?"

"I'm not dead, but I can see ghosts. It seems to be my job to help ghosts who somehow get trapped here in this world to move on."

"Can you help me?"

"I think so." I stood up and looked around. "We'll need your body. Do you remember where you left it?"

The ghost pointed. "It's over there. It's hidden in the dense brush, so you'll need to look carefully."

"Okay. How about I follow you?"

I commanded the dogs to stay, then followed the young woman toward an area of dense forest. She stopped walking when we arrived at a corpse that looked as if it had been dead for at least several days.

"I'm going to call someone to help me," I informed the ghost.

"Do you know who I am?"

I looked around for a purse, wallet, or some form of identification. I didn't want to disturb the corpse, so I hated to go through the victim's pockets. "I don't know who you are. At least not yet. But I'll do my best to find out. Right now, I need to call the police."

The image faded. "Are you still there?"

"I'm here. I don't think we should call the police. I remember trying to avoid the police."

"It's okay. Even if you were running from the police, they can't hurt you now. I need their help to find out who you were."

"Okay. But watch your back. I have a bad feeling about this."

Luckily, the reception in the meadow was good. Also, luckily, Woody was in his office and able to leave immediately to respond to my call. I gave him as detailed directions as I could, then considered my next move. What I really needed was Alyson. "Alyson," I called out to her. "Are you here? Can you hear me?"

I waited for maybe ten seconds before she appeared.

"Alyson this is Josie."

"Are you a ghost too?" Josie asked.

"No. Not a ghost. Is that your body?" Alyson nodded toward the place where Josie had led me.

"Yes."

"What happened?" Alyson asked.

"I'm not sure. I can't really remember."

Alyson looked at me. "Sounds familiar."

"It does. Is Sissy around? Can you get her to join us?" I asked Alyson.

"Maybe. Let me try." Alyson disappeared. Several seconds later, she reappeared with Sissy.

"I know you," Josie said. "You were with me. Before. I remember, you were with me."

Okay, now we were getting somewhere. "Do you happen to remember her name?" I asked Josie.

"Sophia. She said her name was Sophia, though I don't think that was her real name."

"Why do you say that?" I asked.

Josie looked at Sophia. "Every time someone referred to her as Sophia, she looked startled. The name didn't seem to fit her. I think she just made it up, but that's what we called her."

I glanced at Sissy, who had an odd look on her face. "Does Sophia sound right to you?"

"I do remember that name."

"Then that's what we'll call you for now."

"Do you know what happened to us?" Josie asked Sophia.

"No. I can't remember."

"Is your body here too? In these woods?" Josie wondered.

"No. Not here."

"Sophia's body was found in another wooded area about ten miles from here," I explained. "You said you were with Sophia. Do you remember anything about where that was, or if there were others with you?"

Josie began to fade, but then reappeared. "I don't know where we were when we were together. At least not yet, but things are beginning to come back to me. There was another girl. Avery. And there was a man. I think he killed me." Josie looked at Sophia. "He must have killed you too. I wonder if he killed Avery."

That, I thought, was a good question. One I'd need to look into right away. "Do you remember anything from your life before you were with this man?"

Josie tried to think. "No. Not really. There are flashes. I remember swings, and a grassy area. And a cold room with a cement floor. I remember being hungry. When I first found myself in these woods, I didn't remember anything, but I'm starting to get these little pictures that seem to float across my mind."

I glanced at Alyson before I responded. I knew I should encourage Josie to move on, but she might be able to help up identify Sophia and find out who had killed them both. I decided to leave it up to Josie. "Now that your spirit has been liberated from your body, it's important for you to move on to your next life. I'd like to help you do that. Alyson can help as well. But I'd also like to ask you a few more questions before you go. If that's okay with you."

"I'd like to move on. Everything feels wrong here. But I'm willing to help you if I can. What do you want to know?"

"I actually have a lot of questions, but the police are on their way, and they might not understand my ability to talk to you. If it's all right with you, I'd like you to go with Alyson and Sophia. When I'm done here, I'll join you back at our house. I'll ask my questions and then Alyson will help you to the other side."

Josie shrugged. "Okay." She looked at Alyson. "Are you sure you aren't a ghost? You certainly look like one."

"I'm sure. I'll explain along the way."

******

"Two bodies in less than a week," Woody said when he arrived. "This isn't a good trend."

"Trust me, I don't like it any more than you do. This ghost said her name was Josie. She'd been held by the same man who'd held Sophia. That's the first ghost's name. Or at least it might be."

"Might be?"

"Josie said that when she knew her, she was called Sophia, though she thought it might have been a made-up name. Sophia herself didn't know for sure. She remembered being called Sophia, so that's what we're calling her, at least for the time being. Josie said there was a third girl, Avery. She didn't know what happened to her. She didn't remember the name of the man who was holding them or much at all about her life before being in a place she can't remember with the other two girls and the man she thinks killed her."

"Do you think her memories are more accessible than the first victim's?" Woody asked.

"Actually, I do. The spirits of both victims are with Alyson now. Josie indicated she was confused but wanted to move on. I'm going to help her to do that, but first I'm going to see if I can get her to remember more. I think she might be able to tell us who killed both victims, and I'm hoping she might be able to lead us to Avery. It might not be too late for her."

"The fact that one man was holding three girls makes me wonder if there were others as well."

"I had the same thought. I'm hoping Josie's memory will start to return with a nudge."

"That would be helpful. The crime scene unit is on the way. I'll take care of things here if you want to head home. I might stop by later, if that's all right. If you're able to get the second victim to remember more, I may have some questions for her as well."

"Yeah, okay. That would be fine."

"I'll text you before I head over."

As Sunny, Tucker, and I hiked back to the car, I called both Mac and Trevor. Mac was at the house and wasn't planning to go anywhere, so she'd be waiting for me when I got home. Trevor was at work but said he'd get someone to cover for him, then meet us as soon as he was able.

When I arrived at the house, Mac told me she'd talked to Trevor, who planned to be by in an hour or two, so I gave her the condensed version and promised to go over everything in more detail when Trevor arrived. I wanted to speak to my ghost friends alone, so I asked Mac to wait for me while I tried to make contact with Josie and Sophia. I had a feeling Alyson would be in my room, so I headed in that direction. When I got upstairs, I found Josie, Sophia, and Alyson all waiting for me. Apparently, Alyson had introduced Shadow to Josie and Sophia, and both girls were happily petting him. Shadow seemed more than pleased. I suspected Alyson must have introduced Shadow to Sophia before this.

"Did the police know who killed me?" Josie asked.

I sat down on the edge of the bed. "Not yet. But I think we can help them. I know your memories are sketchy, but I'd like to help you remember what you can."

Josie laid back against the pillows. "Okay. What do you want to know?"

"Tell me what you can about what happened to you before your death. Anything at all could be helpful."

"I remember a small room. It was empty except for an old mattress. Sophia and Avery were there with me."

"Do you remember anyone else being there?" I asked.

"No. I think it was just the three of us."

I reached out and ran a hand through Shadow's fur. He began to purr. "Do you know how long you were there?"

Josie shook her head once again. "I don't know. I can't remember."

"Do you remember anything before the room?"

Josie crossed her legs and sat up. "Not really. Like I said, I have a memory of a swing and some grass. I guess I might have been in a park. I remember other empty rooms, all with cement floors. And the smell of decaying garbage. There was something else too. Something warm. And a light." Josie looked at me. "I'm sorry. I can't put all the images together."

"That's okay," I reassured her. "Do you remember anything after the room with the mattress? Anything between being there and realizing you were dead?"

"There was something. There was movement. And a humming."

"A truck," Sophia said. Her eyes seemed to grow wider. "We were in a truck. We were going somewhere with the man."

"That's good." I hoped now that the two were together, they'd be able to help each other remember. "So you were in an empty room for a while and then a truck. Was Avery with you in the truck?"

"Yes," Josie said. "I'm sure we were all together."

I felt confident we were beginning to get somewhere. "I need you both to think back and try to remember where you were after the truck."

Neither ghost responded.

"I don't think they can remember," Alyson said. "I'm not sure they ever will."

Alyson could be correct. Some of the ghosts I'd encountered didn't remember their own deaths, even the ones who remembered everything else.

"Can you tell me anything about the truck?" I asked. "Other than the fact that it was moving. Were you sitting up or laying down? Was it nighttime or day? Did you notice a particular scent? Was it a large truck like a semi or a small pickup?"

"It wasn't a pickup," Sophia said. "It was a big truck without windows. There were no seats in the back, so we had to sit on the floor."

"Yes," Josie said. "I remember that."

"Do either of you have any idea how long you were in the truck?" I figured knowing the length of the ride could help us nail down the place where they'd been held captive.

"It was a long time," Sophia said.

"Yes. More than a day," Josie agreed.

"It was hot," Sophia said. "So hot that I felt sick."

"Do you remember what happened when the truck stopped?"

Sophia's eyes grew big and then she faded away.

"I think you scared her," Josie said.

"I'm sorry. That wasn't my intention."

"I'll see if I can bring her back," Alyson offered.

"It's okay. Let's give her a break." I looked at Josie. "Do *you* remember what happened when the truck stopped?"

"The man took us to a house in the woods."

"Can you tell me where the house was or what it looked like?" I asked.

"I remember wooden floors and a bed. The room had a window, but it was boarded up so we couldn't see out," Josie said. "I think we were locked in the room. I can't remember anything else."

"So the three of you were together in that room in the house in the woods?" I asked.

Josie nodded. "At first. But then the man came and got Sophia. She never came back."

"And you have no idea where he took her?"

"I don't know. He didn't say."

"And after that? Did the man come back? Did he take you somewhere as well?"

Josie put her hand over her eyes. "I don't know. I can't remember."

"That's okay. My friend the policeman is coming by in a while. Why don't we take a break and we'll try again later?"

I headed downstairs to wait for Trevor and Woody. I wanted to find out what had happened to the girls and find the man who had killed them, but I didn't want to push too hard. I didn't want to lose them. Josie seemed more willing to explore her memories, and it seemed both girls had memories that could be accessed, but it might take some time.

I wondered about Avery. Was she here in Cutter's Cove as well? Was she still alive? Might we be able to save her if we could figure out where she was in time? One thing was certain: We needed to try. I could hear someone in the kitchen, probably Mac, so I headed in that direction.

"Any luck?" she asked.

"Some. It seems having both girls together is helping to spark their memories. There were three girls who were all held somewhere together before being put into a truck and taken here. Neither ghost is certain where they were held before that, though."

"So the girls might have been missing for a while."

"Maybe." I grabbed an apple from a bowl. "I wish there was a way to figure out where they were first taken."

"I wonder why the killer brought the girls here. If he kidnapped them elsewhere, why not kill them wherever they were initially being held?"

"Good question, but I have no idea. It does seem odd that someone would hold three girls captive and then take them by truck to a location more than a day away only to kill them." I took a bite of the apple. "Hopefully, Woody will be able to figure out more now that he has two victims to look for."

"Is he coming over?" Mac asked.

"He should be here soon. Once he and Trevor get here, we can have a good, old-fashioned brainstorming session."

******

I went out onto the deck to call Donovan, who told me Jeffery Ryeman from the US Marshal's Portland office would come by to pick up my phone and drop off a new one. Ryeman had been informed about my situation and would be a local resource should I need one. I'd decided to bring Mac and Trevor up to speed but wanted to do so when we were together. I realized Mac would wonder what was going on when someone from the US Marshal's pulled up, so I told her that I was providing the man with information about my time in witness protection and left it at that. Geez, when it rained, it really did pour.

******

As it turned out, it was dinnertime by the time Woody and Trevor arrived. Trevor brought a couple pizzas and Mac made a salad while I took the dogs out for a quick run. I hadn't spoken to either Josie or Sophia since that afternoon, but I hoped if I allowed some time to pass, they'd remember more on their own.

"The ME is estimating Josie Gomez died three or four days after the victim we're calling Sophia," Woody began.

"So Josie has been positively identified?" I asked.

He nodded. "She disappeared from Waco, Texas, four years ago at the age of sixteen. Her parents filed a missing persons report at the time. It was assumed she had run away, but that was never confirmed. As far as I can tell, Josie hadn't been seen by anyone who knew her since before she was reported missing."

"It sounds like maybe she didn't run away at all," Trevor said. "She might have been kidnapped."

"That's a possibility," Woody confirmed. "But four years is a long time to be held by a kidnapper. It's more likely she ran away and left Waco, and then was taken by the man who killed her."

"Even if she wasn't still living in Waco when she was taken, at least we have a name now. Maybe that will help us identify the other two."

"Maybe. At least it gives us a starting point."

"So what do we know about Josie?" I asked. "I'm curious as to why she might have been singled out by the man who kidnapped and then killed her."

"Josie was a troubled teen. She was the youngest of seven children and seemed to have tried to make herself stand out by participating in questionable activity. By the time she was sixteen, she had been arrested four times. Little things: petty theft, vandalism, that sort of thing. She cut school on a regular basis and could often be found smoking pot in the park with her older friends."

"She mentioned swings and grass," I said. "I wonder if she was taken from the park."

"Possibly," Woody answered. "It's hard to be sure what happened to her. All we know for certain is that at some point, Josie failed to go home. When her parents couldn't find her and none of her friends admitted to having seen her, they filed a missing persons report. At the time, the opinion was that she'd run away. It appears some effort was made to find her, but given her age and history, I don't think it was much."

"Okay, so there are two possibilities: that Josie was taken from Waco four years ago and was held all that time or that she did run away and was taken from wherever it was she wound up."

"I think we should consider both."

"It sort of fits that a predator might have been on the lookout for troubled kids like Josie. Maybe we should look for individuals in and around Waco who might fit Sophia's description with police records similar to Josie's."

"I did that when I first got the lead about Waco. Nothing popped, but I think the idea is worth exploring, so I'll widen my search to other locations. If Josie ran away and met up with Sophia and the killer outside Texas, it will make things harder, but all three girls being runaways is possible. I've asked myself a dozen times why I haven't been able to find a missing persons report associated with Sophia. If she did run away and her parents or guardian knew it, they might not even have bothered to report it. Especially if she was a problem teen they might almost have been glad to be rid of."

I placed my hand on my heart. The very idea of being unwanted by ones' parents made it hurt.

"I'd like to come back to the fact that Josie and Sophia appeared to have been killed by the same person yet they died at least a few days apart and in different locations," Mac said. "Why?"

Woody shook his head. "I have no idea. He may have had a specific reason to bring the girls to Cutter's Cove that isn't yet apparent."

Mac looked at me. "Maybe you should try to talk to them again. I know you wanted to give them a break, but if there's another girl out there who may still be alive, we need to figure this out sooner rather than later."

"I'll go up and have another chat with them while the three of you continue to work on piecing together what we do know."

As I had before, when I arrived in my bedroom, I found both Josie and Sophia on the bed with Shadow. Alyson was watching from a spot near the window.

"I saw the police officer is here," Josie said. "Did he figure out what happened to me?"

"Some of it," I confirmed. "It appears you were twenty years old, the youngest of seven children, and lived in Waco, Texas. It seems you had a police record by the time you disappeared when you were sixteen. Most assumed you ran away, but that was never confirmed."

"That feels familiar. I used to cut school and hang out in the park with my friends."

"That's right," I said. "Have you remembered anything else?"

"I met a guy. Blade. He was going to Los Angeles and I decided to tag along."

"Did you make it to LA?" I asked.

"Yes, we did. But something happened to Blade after we got there. I remember being alone. And scared. But then I met some people and things got a little better."

"What people?"

"Street people. There were places I could go where runaways like me hung out. It wasn't perfect, but it was better than going home."

So far, this was making sense. Runaway kids living on the street would make perfect prey for someone looking for victims who wouldn't be missed by anyone. "Do you remember what happened before you ended up in the room with Sophia and Avery?" I asked.

Josie shook her head. "No, but I'm beginning to remember living on the streets. Begging for money for food and huddling with the other homeless people I'd met around a garbage can fire. I can remember wanting to find a way off the streets, but not what happened next."

"Do you remember meeting the man who killed you?"

"No."

"Do you remember whether he hurt you after he kidnapped you?"

"He killed me," Josie pointed out.

I let out a breath. "Yes. I know. I guess what I'm asking is whether he assaulted you. Physically or sexually. I'm trying to understand why he took you in the first place."

Josie faded away. I looked around for Sophia, but she was gone as well. I turned to Alyson.

"Sophia left a while ago," Alyson informed me. "I'd give her some time to regroup. Josie too."

"I guess I was pushing kind of hard. I'll go talk to the others. We're still hoping to find Avery before it's too late."

"Do you think she's still alive?"

I shrugged. "Probably not, but one can hope."

I rejoined the others, and Woody said he'd begin to look for traces of Sophia in Los Angeles. If Josie had been living on the streets there when she was kidnapped by the man who held and eventually killed her, maybe Sophia was as well. Woody had a friend who was a PI in Orange County, and we decided to hire him to take photos of Josie and Sophia, which Woody would provide, and begin to show them around in the homeless communities. We knew finding someone who recognized them in a huge place like LA would be like finding a needle in a haystack, but we thought it was worth the time and expense to at least try.

Once Woody left, I informed Mac and Trevor that I had something else to speak to them about. "Now don't freak out," I started after we sat back down in the living room.

"This doesn't sound good," Trevor said.

"It's not a big deal. At least, I don't think it is," I answered. "I just received some news I wanted to share with my two best friends. After all the secrets I had to keep the last time I lived here, I want to assure you I have a new policy of open and honest communication."

Mac looked at Trevor. "You're right. This has to be bad." Mac looked at me. "Just spit it out."

"I got a text the other day, which is why the marshal was here today."

"Marshal?" Trevor asked.

"Jeffery Ryeman, from the US Marshal's office in Portland. He came by to pick up my phone and leave me a new one. I'll give you both the number."

"What about the text?" Mac asked.

I shared the content of the text, and that the man Donovan had been certain must have sent it couldn't have.

"So there's some new wacko with a vendetta against you?" Trevor asked.

"Maybe." I blew out a breath. I guess I was tenser than I wanted to admit. "We don't know a lot, and there was only the one text. It could have been just a prank."

"A prank?" Trevor asked. "Who would even have the knowledge required to pull off something like that other than individuals who aren't likely to waste their time pranking anyone?"

He had a point. The text was most likely a threat and not a prank.

"Are you in danger?" Mac asked. "Should we hide you?"

"Donovan has no reason to believe I'm in any immediate danger. The text went to a New York City phone number. Chances are whoever sent it has no idea I'm not still there. I promised to keep my eyes open and Donovan promised to keep his ear to the ground. I don't think there's an imminent threat to anyone, but I wanted you both to know what was going on. And Mac, if you'd be more comfortable staying with Trevor, I totally understand."

"I'm not going anywhere," Mac said. "Although I may finally get a gun and learn to shoot it. I've been thinking about it for a while."

"Just be sure you don't shoot me if I get up for a glass of water in the middle of the night." I tried for a light tone, but I think it came off as terrified, which, I assured myself, I wasn't.

"I should stay here too," Trevor said.

"There's no need for that," I said. "I have an alarm system, two dogs, and solid locks. I'm probably safest in the house." I took a deep breath. "Look, guys, I've been through this before. The last time was a bit more intense because there were definitely men after me and not just some vague threat, but the situation took two years to be resolved. If there's a real threat now—and I'm not saying there is—it could take months or even years to finally come to a head. I can't live my life based on what may or may not happen. Yes, I can take precautions, and I will. But for all we know, the text was sent by someone who just wanted to scare me."

"There aren't a lot of people who know about the Bonatello brothers and their relationship to you other than the Bonatellos themselves," Trevor reminded me.

"True. But the Bonatellos are a family. There are a lot of members. I don't think it's outside the realm of possibility to think someone—maybe a cousin or an uncle—knew about my role in the death of Mario and Clay and have decided to scare me. I'll admit that the fact that Franco is dead and Vito is in charge concerns me. But what am I supposed to do? Let Donovan put me into witness protection again, if I even qualify?"

"No. I don't think that's the answer," Trevor acknowledged.

"So work with me on this. Be there to act as a sounding board when I need one, and watch my back, but don't freak out and don't suffocate me."

Trevor made a face, but I noticed he didn't agree to my request. Mac, on the other hand, got up and hugged me. She told me she was there for me and then said good night and headed up to bed. Trevor said good night as well, but as he left, I had the feeling that letting this go wasn't something he was going to be willing or able to do.

Chapter 4

Saturday, October 27

As we did almost every morning, the dogs and I got up early and headed out for our walk. It was overcast today and the temperature was definitely on the chilly side, but so far, the air was dry and the breeze blowing in from the west was no more than a whisper. As I did most mornings, I used the time to enjoy the beauty around me and mentally prepare for my day. I was determined not to obsess over the text I'd received. It had been five days and I hadn't heard another thing. Maybe I wouldn't. I knew if I let it, the text could completely occupy my every thought, so I decided I would push any concerns I might have to the back of my mind and concentrate on Josie and Sophia and the madman who'd killed them.

I planned to speak to them again today. My sense was that Josie was ready to move on, and it wouldn't be right to detain her no matter how much I wanted her help in identifying Sophia and possibly finding Avery. After I spoke to her today, I'd offer her the option, and if she wanted to go, I'd let her. Alyson had assured me that she was happy to get her started in the right direction.

In addition to the sleuthing activities I had planned, tonight was also the masquerade ball. I had a killer dress I couldn't wait to wear, so come hell or high water, I intended to wrap up my investigating for the day in time to spend at least a couple of hours getting ready. I just hoped the investigation into the deaths of the two girls didn't prevent Woody from being able to attend. The last thing I wanted was to be a fifth wheel accompanying Trevor, Mac, and their dates.

I was standing on the edge of the bluff looking out to sea when Alyson appeared. "Sophia remembered something."

"Great." I smiled at Alyson. "What?"

"She was in LA before she was abducted too. She doesn't remember why she was there, or anything about her life before that, but she does remember the traffic and the crowded streets and being in a car with a cop and then waking up in a room with a mattress on the floor."

A policeman? Could he be the killer? If so, that would be an interesting twist.

"So Sophia was in a car with a cop, which may have meant she'd been arrested. Did she remember going to jail?"

"No. Just being in a car and then being taken to the room where she was held until she was brought north."

"So maybe the cop is the one who kidnapped and killed her."

"It seems he was. It's starting to come back to her, but it's still fuzzy. She doesn't think Sophia was her real name. She remembers being called that, but it doesn't feel right. She's still trying to remember who she was before she ended up in LA, but it's a complete blank."

"Did she tell you any specifics about her time in LA? Where she lived? Who she hung out with?"

"Not yet, but my sense is that her memory is slowly coming back."

I smiled. "That's great. I need to talk to her."

"There's more. After Sophia told me she was arrested before she woke up in the room with the mattress, Josie remembered a policeman as well. She said she and a group of homeless people had set up camp in an abandoned building. Someone must have called the cops, because they showed up and threatened to arrest everyone. In the end, they let everyone go, but the policeman told her that she had to go with him because she had priors. Like Sophia, she said the next thing she remembered was waking up in the room with the mattress."

"Did either girl tell you anything about the cop? His name or what he looked like?"

"They didn't remember a name, but they both said he had dark hair and dark eyes."

That didn't narrow things down much, but it was something. I thanked Alyson and headed back to the house. First, I needed to call Woody; then, I needed to try to talk to both girls to see if I could eek out any additional information. After that, I needed to chat with them about their desire to stay or move on.

Mac was up and the coffee was made by the time I returned to the house. I poured myself a cup and settled at the dining table overlooking the sea. I sent a quick text to Woody letting him know I had news and asking him to call me when he had a minute.

"Looks like you've jumped right into your day," Mac commented after I set my phone aside.

"Alyson met me out on the bluff to let me know both girls remembered having an experience with a cop right before they woke up in the dark room."

"You think they were kidnapped by a cop?"

"It's beginning to look that way. Josie told Alyson she'd been squatting in an abandoned building and someone called the cops, and Sophia remembered being in a car with a cop but doesn't know why. They both were in LA when it happened. I feel like we're finally getting close to figuring this out."

Mac took a sip of her coffee, then said, "If a cop kidnapped and killed these girls, it makes me wonder if there were others."

"I had the same thought," I admitted.

Mac took another sip of her coffee and swallowed it slowly. "So why, if this cop kidnapped these girls in LA, did he bring them to Cutter's Cove to kill them?"

I frowned. "That part really doesn't make sense. There must have been a reason for him to bring them here. Even if he didn't want to kill the girls and dump the bodies in LA for some reason, there's a lot of geography between LA and here."

"Knowing why he came here might help us figure out where he is now. I can't get the third girl out of my mind. Knowing there's a possibility she could still be alive makes things feel a lot more urgent to me."

"I agree. I want Sophia and Josie to find their answers, but if Avery is alive, finding her before it's too late has to be our priority."

"Cutter's Cove is a small town. Maybe we should be looking for a truck with California plates. Maybe something that's been parked at a hotel or motel for the past couple of weeks."

"He wouldn't take the girls somewhere so public," I said. "Besides, they remembered being held in a cabin in the woods. If I was going to rent a space in which I intended to kill my victims, I think I'd rent one of the forest service cabins up in the mountains."

"That would be a good place to hide. And both bodies were found in the woods. I bet if we use the two burial sites as pinpoints, we can figure out a search area."

"Let's use the points to set up a parameter, then take a look to see if we can find the truck the guy was driving."

Mac went into her office to work her magic on the computer. Using the two burial sites as starting points, she set up a search grid, then cross-referenced that with known roads and cabin rentals. She was going to set up specific GPS points for us to follow so we would be able to cover the largest area possible given the limited amount of time we'd allotted ourselves.

Trevor was on his way over to help out as well. I'd decided not to bring the dogs along. They'd enjoy the trip, but I wasn't sure what we'd find and I didn't want to put them in danger should we find a cold-blooded killer. I'd spoken to Woody, so he knew what we were planning to do. He warned me more than once to call him if we found anything suspect and not to engage in any way until he arrived. I promised him we'd be careful and assured him big-time danger wasn't what I was after on this particular Saturday.

Once Mac had a plan and Trevor had shown up with the snacks, we set out in his truck to the spot we'd chosen as the best starting point. Trevor appeared to be in a good mood and didn't bring up our conversation of the previous evening. Maybe he really did plan to let me call the shots, which made sense, considering it was my text and my life. Of course, I knew that what affected me affected the people who loved me. I needed to remember that.

Our plan was a simple one. We intended to drive up and down all the roads streets that serviced the cabins dotted around the area. Some were seasonal units only accessible by dirt road, so when we got to the area where the most isolated cabins were located, we'd park the truck and walk. If we tried to drive those dirt roads, the dust we stirred up would destroy the element of surprise, which was the only thing we had going for us.

"Most of the cabins are already boarded up for the season," Mac said as we drove slowly up one narrow road and down the next.

"The area is pretty deserted," Trevor agreed. "We've been driving around for an hour and haven't passed a single car."

"Which means this would be the perfect location for a killer to be hanging out," I pointed out.

"Agreed," Trevor said. "We should make note of any occupied cabins. We can text a list to Woody, and then he or his men can check them out."

I pulled out the map Mac had printed off. I considered the topography as well as the places she'd indicated cabins were located. It was likely the killer had ditched the truck if he was still around. Given the fact that at least two of the three girls we believed had been with him were dead, it was even more likely he was long gone.

"The cabin at the end of that dead-end road has smoke coming out of the chimney," Trevor said as he slowed the truck.

"It backs up to the forest, and if you hike in a southeasterly direction, you'll come to the waterfall trail where we found the first body after about a mile," Mac added.

"It seems that cabin is a real possibility," Trevor agreed. "Having said that, although it's late in the season, there are still people who come up here to get away from it all, so it could be occupied by a family on a weekend getaway."

"What should we do?" Mac asked. "I hate to have Woody running out here for every single cabin we find occupied, and there's no trace of a truck, or any vehicle at all for that matter."

"Let's just note the location on the map. Woody can follow up later," I suggested.

"Hang on," Trevor said as the front door began to open.

I couldn't help but hold my breath as the door opened fully and a large black dog bounded out, followed by a couple who looked to be in their twenties. They called to the dog and headed to the trail leading to the falls.

"I don't think there's a killer staying there," Mac said.

I frowned. "No. But let's mark the cabin on the map anyway. Maybe we should have a code: green for occupied but highly unlikely to house the killer, yellow for occupied but occupant couldn't be established, and red for any cabin that seems suspicious for some reason."

"Good idea," Mac said. She was sitting between Trevor and me on the truck's bench seat. She opened the map and pointed to a cluster of cabins up a side road we'd passed on the way to our current location. "Let's check over there. The road's narrow and windy, so it's unlikely anyone drove a panel truck up there, but if the killer dumped the truck, it would make a really good place to hide out. And it's closer to the waterfall trail on foot."

"Okay," Trevor said, making a U-turn. "It's worth a look."

As Mac had predicted, the road was one hairpin turn after another, preventing Trevor from driving faster than a few miles an hour or so. Although the cabins weren't all that far from the main road, it was taking us forever to travel it. I'd had a tendency toward car sickness when I was a kid, so I cracked the window a bit just to be safe.

"I think the first of the row of cabins will be just up here on the left," Mac said.

Trevor slowed even more. The first cabin we came to was boarded up, as was the second and third. The fourth looked to be occupied based on the fishing equipment out on the front deck. We didn't want to be too obvious, so we continued past it before Trevor pulled over and stopped.

"There were at least four poles leaning against the side of the cabin," Trevor said. "That says to me it's a guys' trip to the mountains, not a serial killer."

"Yeah," I agreed. "I'd still like to get a peek inside, though. Maybe we can find a place to park off the road, then circle back and take a peek in the window."

"Sounds dangerous," Mac said.

"Not if the cabin really is occupied by a group of guys on a fishing trip," I said.

"Just mark the cabin with a yellow dot as we discussed," Trevor said as he began to slowly make his way up the road. "None of us need to take chances or be heroes today."

It was best to stick to the plan, but that didn't mean my natural need to know rather than suspect wasn't getting the better of me. Again, this would be a good time for Alyson, who could take a peek without being in any danger, to show up. Unfortunately, she didn't magically appear as she had on other occasions when I'd needed her.

It didn't take long to complete our search of the area. We identified two additional cabins that appeared to have occupants. Neither showed activity while we were there, but there were cars parked out front of both. We assumed the renters were out hiking and marked both cabins with a yellow dot.

Our next area to search was a cluster of rustic cabins that could be reached by a rutted dirt road. It was at the access point to these cabins that we decided to park and walk. And after all the driving around on narrow, windy roads, I was ready for a walk.

"There are six cabins along this road," Mac reported. "They're spread out and tucked into the forest. It should be easy to sneak up and take a peek without being seen." Mac got out the map and took a closer look. "The first cabin is on the left, about an eighth of a mile up. If we stay on the road, we should see a narrow dirt drive. I haven't been up here since I was a kid, but I'm pretty sure most of the cabins can't be seen from the road, which means we'll need to walk through the forest to get a look at each one."

"That's fine with me," I said. "A walk will be nice."

"I have some binoculars in my backpack," Trevor said. "We'll take them so we can get a good look without having to get too close."

It took us about forty minutes to check the first three cabins. Only one, the first, was occupied. A peek through the binoculars revealed two men sitting on the front deck drinking beer. The way they were dressed indicated to us that they'd just come back from fishing.

"The next two cabins are pretty close to each other," Mac said after consulting her map. "In fact, they share the same drive. I doubt a killer would have rented one of them, but I suppose they're worth a look."

The first cabin appeared to be empty, but the second had a truck in the drive. It was a pickup, though, and the girls had made it sound as if they were in a panel truck without windows. The last cabin in the area, which was the most isolated, at the top of the road, had a black panel truck parked in the drive. From the description the girls had given me, it could have been the truck the girls remembered.

"We need to get a peek inside," I whispered.

"We need to call Woody," Trevor countered.

I blew out a breath. "Okay. We'll call Woody." I looked at my phone. "No bars."

"My satellite phone will work," Mac said. "I just need to walk down the road a bit to a spot where there are fewer trees."

"Okay, let's go," I said. "The sooner we get this guy, the better."

It was almost an hour before Woody arrived with two of his men. Mac, Trevor, and I were instructed to wait back where we'd left Trevor's truck. I was about to argue, but a stern look from the suddenly intimidating cop all decked out in his bullet-proof vest, had me agreeing to whatever he requested.

"Do you think the guy is still there?" Mac said, as we walked back to the truck.

"We watched the place for an hour while we waited for Woody and I didn't see any evidence the cabin was occupied."

"Yeah," Mac agreed. "It looked pretty deserted."

"Maybe he was just sleeping," Trevor suggested.

"Or maybe we were too late and he was out killing the third girl." Mac groaned.

"Or maybe he was never there at all and the truck belongs to someone else," I said.

"The truck has Oregon plates," Trevor provided. "Hadn't we pretty much decided the killer drove the girls from California?"

"Unless the plates were stolen," Mac added.

Trevor lowered the tailgate to his truck and we all jumped up and had a seat.

"I really hate waiting," I complained.

Trevor wound his fingers through mine. "I know. Me too. But it won't be long now."

And it was less than thirty minutes later when Woody showed up to let us know that the truck was most likely the one that had brought the girls to Cutter's Cove. Inside the cabin was a room with a boarded-up window and a bed, just as the girls had described it. It was empty now, but there was blood on the mattress, which made it seem obvious someone had been kept and hurt there at some point. Woody had already called for CSI people to carefully process the entire cabin. Given the complex nature of the investigation, Woody was pretty sure he wouldn't be able to join us for the limo ride to the masquerade ball, though he'd try to meet us there if he could. I told him to focus on finding the madman who had killed at least two girls and might be holding a third and not to worry about the ball.

We headed back to my house. I wanted to fill Alyson and the ghosts in on what we'd found, and to offer them the help we'd promised to move on if they were ready. I had the feeling Josie would take us up on it, but Sophia might want to stay. Both had recovered part of their memory, but Josie knew who she had been in life, while Sophia still wondered.

******

"We found the cabin where you were held," I informed the two ghosts as soon as I got home and asked Alyson to bring them to my room. "It was empty, but the police are searching for evidence. I hoped you might have remembered more about what happened to you now that you've had more time to think about things."

"I remember," Josie said. She looked at Sophia, who faded away.

"Are you willing to share it with me?"

Josie nodded. "I've already told you I was living on the streets in LA when I was arrested for trespassing. What I didn't remember before was that the cop who arrested me offered me a deal when we were alone in his car."

"What sort of a deal?" I asked.

"He said he was part of a team who was filming a reality show, and they needed contestants. If I agreed to be part of it, he'd forget I had a bunch of priors and let me go. I'd seen shows like *Survivor* and thought that would be a lot better than going to jail, so I agreed. He took me to this little house in the Valley. We were supposed to wait there for a few days until the others arrived. I didn't question it. He was a cop and he was offering me an out, so I told him it was fine. He made me some food, which I ate, and when I woke up I was in the room with the mattress. I thought it was weird, but I wondered if being locked in the room was some sort of a test."

"And then?"

"I didn't have to wait long, maybe a day, before Sophia showed up. Like me, she was arrested and, like me, she was offered an out if she agreed to participate in a reality show. Neither of us liked being locked in a room without any furniture, but food and water was brought to us, and we were allowed to come out one at a time to use the bathroom, so we waited to see what would happen. A day or two later, Avery showed up. Shortly after that, we were put into the truck and taken to a cabin in the woods. As we had been before, we were locked in a room, but at least this one had a bed."

"That sounds like the cabin we just found. It's empty now. What happened after you arrived?"

"I guess a day or two passed before the policeman, who was wearing fatigues, not a uniform, came into the room and told us the game was going to start. He took Sophia with him and left Avery and me behind. We waited for Sophia to come back, but she never did. After a few more days, the policeman show up again in his fatigues and told me it was my turn. I was scared because I didn't know what had happened to Sophia, but I didn't really have a choice. We hiked out into the woods for a while. Once we were at least a mile away from the cabin, he told me that we were going to play the hunting game."

I felt my stomach lurch as I realized what was coming next.

"He told me," Josie continued, "he would give me an hour head start and then come looking for me. I knew he planned to shoot me when he found me, so I ran. I hoped the hour head start would be enough, but it wasn't. I didn't know where I was or have a plan, so I probably just ran in circles. I'm not sure how long I ran before I heard the gunshot and everything went black. The next thing I knew, I was standing over my body."

"Oh God. I'm so very sorry. That must have been terrifying."

"It wasn't fun." Josie let out a sigh that sounded more like a growl. "What's done is done. He can't hurt me anymore. No one can. I know you want my help to catch him, but I don't remember anything else. Sophia doesn't remember as much as I do, though she's just starting to remember. Maybe she can help you find him. I should stay to help, but this is all too depressing. I don't remember being happy when I was alive and I'm certainly not happy as a ghost. I think I'm ready to move on to what I hope will be a happier place."

"And you should. Alyson will help you. Thank you for staying as long as you did. I'm sure this has been very hard on you." I glanced at Alyson.

"Are you ready?" Alyson asked.

Josie nodded.

Alyson took her hand and the two disappeared.

I felt we were beginning to get a handle on what had happened to the girls, but we still didn't know who the killer was and, even more important, what had become of Avery.

******

"Wow," I said to Mac when I walked into her bedroom, where she was getting ready for the ball. "You look… wow." I hugged my hands to my chest as I tried to find the words to convey how beautiful she looked. "You look amazing."

Mac glanced nervously in the mirror. "You don't think it's too much?"

I shook my head as I considered the dark green dress that hugged Mac's figure in a way that left no doubt that beneath the somewhat plain and serviceable clothes she usually wore was a woman with a killer body. "I think it's perfect. I love the design and the color. It really brings out the green in your eyes. You look amazing and Ty, who's here, by the way, is going to totally lose it when he sees you."

Mac crossed her arms over her breasts. "You don't think it's too revealing?"

I reached out and put my hands on Mac's arms to pull them to her sides. "I think it's absolutely perfect. The dress is perfect, the hair is perfect, the makeup is perfect; everything's all just perfect."

"Okay." Mac let out a long sigh. "You look beautiful, as always. Is Woody still tied up?"

I nodded. "For now. It's fine, though. It's much more important to find the man who killed those girls."

"And Trevor?"

"He texted that he's on his way to pick up Brooklyn, and then he'll have the limo swing by to pick us up."

Mac turned to look in the full-length mirror again. "With the way things turned out, it might have been better not to have badgered Trevor into bringing a date."

I shrugged. "Yeah. You might have a point there."

Mac caught my eyes in the mirror. "But it'll still be fun. For all of us. Just a bunch of friends attending a charity event."

I couldn't help but grin at Mac's nervousness. "Yes," I said with conviction. "It's going to be fun. Now, let's go down and show you off. You, my dear, are definitely going to be the belle of the ball."

And she was. At least in Ty's eyes. After seeing the couple melt into each other on the dance floor, I was pretty sure the just-friends status Mac had been insisting on was a thing of the past. They moved as if they were made for each other. I envied them the perfect synchronicity they shared. I'd had several long-term relationships in my life, but none of the men I'd dated had seemed to fit me the way Mac and Ty fit each other.

"Would you like to dance?" Trevor, who looked handsome in his tux, asked.

"Where's your date? Did she ditch you already?" I teased.

"Apparently." Trevor chuckled as he nodded to the dance floor, where Brooklyn was dancing with the man who'd taken over the job of high school football coach.

I shrugged. "Her loss." I put my hand on Trevor's arm and let him lead me out onto the dance floor, where he pulled me into his arms and began to sway ever so slightly. I'd known Trevor since we were teenagers, but we'd never slow danced before tonight. It was nice. More than nice. It was … Well, it was something I promised myself I wouldn't think about. At least not in relation to Trevor. Still, it was hard to keep my pulse under control with Trev's strong hand on my bare back and his warm breath on my neck.

Deciding I needed to break the sexual tension between us, I did the only thing I could think of; I began to babble. "If I knew how well you cleaned up, I might have taken you out dancing before this."

Trevor pulled back just a bit so we were eye to eye. "Any time you want to go dancing, I'm your man. Keep in mind, though, this is my one and only move. I didn't even have this one until this week."

"You learned to dance this week?"

"Mac gave me lessons. I realized after I asked Brooklyn to the ball, I'd never learned to dance. She took pity on me and showed me a few things. I remember this, and only this."

This, I decided, was pretty darn good as Trevor's body swayed in time with mine. "You know," I said as I pulled him just a bit closer, "I'm an excellent dancer. Ballroom dancing is one of the things kids from my neck of the woods learn at an early age. If you think you might want to add a few more moves to your repertoire, I'd be happy to teach you. For a price, that is."

"Price?" Trevor raised a brow.

"I'm thinking a latte and scone delivered to my deck every morning for a week should suffice."

Trevor grinned. "Deal."

Chapter 5

Sunday, October 28

When Trevor showed up with a latte and a scone the next morning, I had to laugh. "After our late night, I wasn't expecting you today. You must really want those dance lessons."

"Oh, I do. I've thought about it and I'm all in. I want to learn the waltz, the rumba, the foxtrot, and let's not forget the most sensual dance of all, the tango."

I took a sip of my latte. "We'll start with a waltz and see how it goes. Right now, however, I need to take Tucker and Sunny out for their morning walk. Want to come with us?"

"Sure."

"We'll bring the lattes and leave the scones for when we get back."

"If you don't want Mac to eat the scones, you might want to hide them," Trevor warned. "I brought a half dozen, but you know what a sweet tooth she has."

I glanced toward the stairs. "I have a feeling Mac and Ty might not be up for a while yet. If I had to guess, I'd say their night was only getting started when we got home."

Trevor glanced toward the stairs as well. "Really? Good for Mac. It's about time she found herself a guy who's worthy of her affection. I hope this will be the beginning of something awesome."

I called to the dogs and we all headed to the front door. "I really like Ty, and he seems to adore Mac. And they have a lot in common with all that computer stuff. I think they could have a real future together. Of course, I'm enjoying having her as a roommate, so I'm not quite ready for Ty to steal her out from under me. By the way, speaking of things that are stolen, I'm sorry Brooklyn decided to go home with the football coach."

Trevor shrugged. "I was fine with it. It was never really a date. I only invited her because you wanted me to invite someone and she came to mind."

"The evening didn't go exactly as I'd planned, but I had a good time, and I think Chelsea made a ton of money for the hospital."

"She told me that they almost doubled their goal amount. Seems like everyone was in a giving mood. I bought some thingamabob for a ridiculous amount of money."

"A thingamabob?"

"I'm not sure what it is. You might hang it on a wall. Or set it on a desk. It might even be for a bathroom."

I laughed. "You paid a lot of money for something you don't even know what to do with?"

"Had to. Chelsea grabbed me when I went to get us some wine. She told me to bid on something, so I bid on the thing nearest to me at the time. Apparently, my bid was crazy high, but the money went to a good cause, so I'm fine with it. How about you? Did you buy anything?"

"I did. Although unlike you, I know what I bought and am very happy with my purchases. Oh look." I pointed. "Dolphins."

"You don't see them every day," Trevor said as we paused to watch them jumping in the waves.

"They certainly look like they're having fun," I responded. "I can't wait for winter, when the whales are most active. I can remember sitting on the deck overlooking the water as they breached and splashed off the coastline. Remember that one December—I think it was the year before I left—when we saw the whales feeding in the waves under the full moon?"

"You and Mac and I built a fire in the pit despite the fact that it was freezing. We were huddled under a pile of blankets while we watched the show." Trevor put his arm around my shoulders. "Those really were good times."

"They were. I'm so happy to be back. And don't even get me started on the holidays. Will you be in town for Thanksgiving and Christmas, or are you going to see your family?"

"I'll be here. I close the restaurant on Thanksgiving Day, as well as Christmas Eve and

Christmas Day. This year Christmas is on a Tuesday. We're closed on Monday anyway, so I'm going to close on Sunday too, so my entire staff can have a three-day weekend."

"That's great. If you'll be in town, you're invited to have Thanksgiving and Christmas with Mac and me. I have a feeling Ty will be here as well. And Mom is coming back for Christmas." I leaned my head on Trevor's shoulder. "We'll have the best time. I may even risk life and limb to go to the Christmas Carnival. They do still have it?"

"They do. And I'm pretty sure no one has done anything about maintenance on the Ferris wheel since you almost fell to your death, so we have that to look forward to."

I felt myself relax as a wave of contentment washed over me. It was good to be home.

"I'm not pushing and I'm not prying, but is there any news on the other front?" Trevor asked.

"If you mean the text, no. If another one comes through, the marshal's office will pick it up on my old phone. I'm not sure what will happen. I guess Donovan will be notified, and he'll contact me." I turned and looked at Trevor. "I know you're worried. But this is one of those situations where there isn't anything I can do about it. I could worry and fret, but where would that get me?"

"You're right. I know you're right. And you've been through something just like this before, so you know how to handle yourself. It's just that I care about you." Trevor used a finger to wipe away a stray hair that had blown across my face. He looked me directly in the eye. "I lost you once. I don't know what I'd do if I lost you again."

I didn't know what to say, so I didn't say anything. Instead, I put my arms around him and hugged him as tightly as I could. After several minutes, Sunny interrupted us, and we decided to head back. As we rounded the front drive, Woody pulled up in his squad car. He saw us and waved, then parked. Trevor volunteered to take the dogs inside, so I walked over to join Woody as he exited his car.

"You're out and about early this morning," I said with a smile.

"It's been a tough week. I guess my regular schedule is skewed a bit. I didn't even realize how early it was when I pulled into your drive as I made my way back into town along the highway. I hope it isn't too early."

"You're fine. Do you want to come in?"

He glanced at the house. "No. I was driving to my office, and I really should continue on. I pulled in when I realized I was going to travel right past your house and thought I'd fill you in."

"I'm glad you did. I've been wondering how everything was going. Is there any progress?"

"I don't know if I'd call it progress exactly, but there have been developments. After we spoke yesterday, I shared the story Josie told you with the medical examiner, although I presented it as a hypothetical scenario, not as the testimony of a ghost."

"And…?"

"And based on the injuries incurred and the physical evidence found on the body, running through the woods before being shot in the back fit the injuries on the body. In addition, it appeared Josie fell and got up several times in her mad dash away from the killer."

I put my hand to my chest. "Those poor girls. I can't even imagine how terrifying it must be to know someone is chasing you with the intention to kill you."

"Finding the third girl is the top priority for me, although I imagine she's probably dead. The other two died within a few days of each other."

"I'd have to agree, considering the fact that the cabin was empty, and it's been more than a week since the first victim died. Still, I'd like to find her body, and I want to help Sophie find her answers, and, naturally, I want to see the killer behind bars before he has the chance to hurt anyone else. Did you find any prints in the truck?"

"The cab was wiped clean, but they found some prints and DNA evidence in the back of the truck. We might be able to get an ID on the driver, but I kind of doubt it. The guy seemed pretty careful. We can use what we found to prove the two victims we have in the morgue were actually in the truck. It may even help us identify Avery and Sophia."

Well, that was something, I supposed. "I'll talk to Sophia again. She tends to fade away if I push too hard, but maybe I can get her to open up a bit. She might remember something Josie didn't. She might even be able to help us ID the killer."

"I'm going on to the station to dig through old incident and arrest reports. I keep thinking I'll stumble across something that links back to Sophia. It would be good to positively identify her."

"Call me if you find anything, and I'll call you if Sophia remembers anything Josie didn't already tell me."

After Woody left, I went inside and up to my room. I didn't see either Sophia or Alyson, so I called to both and waited. I had the feeling at least part of Sophia's amnesia was intentional. Not that I blamed her. If what had happened to her had happened to me, I wouldn't want to remember either.

"What's up?" Alyson asked when she appeared.

I frowned. "Don't you know what's up? I thought you know what I know."

"Only when we're merged. I've been with Sophia since you found her in the woods, so I haven't been with you. I'm sorry I missed the ball. How was it?"

"It was fine. We made a lot of money for the hospital."

"I didn't mean that," Alyson said. "How was the rest? Was your dress a hit? Did you have fun with Woody? Did you dance with Trevor?"

"My dress was well received, Woody was unable to attend due to the discovery of the cabin in the woods, and I did dance with Trevor."

Alyson began to float around the room as if she were dancing. "Was it dreamy? I bet it was dreamy."

"Can we put talk of the dance on hold for a bit? I need to talk to Sophia. Is she around? Can you bring her to me?"

"She's around, but I have to warn you, she's pretty freaked out. If you're going to try to make her remember again, you need to take it slow. She's really traumatized."

I took a breath. "I know. If she went through the same thing Josie did, I can't believe how horrific it must have been. I hate to ask her to try to remember, but if there's any possibility she can help us find the man who did this to her and the others, I have to try. We still don't know what became of Avery, and it's possible there are others waiting for their turn to play this guy's sick, sick game."

"I know. I'll try to get her to come to you." Alyson looked at Shadow. "She might want to see the cat."

I waited for about ten minutes before Alyson reappeared, alone. "Sorry. I'd give it some more time."

"Yeah, okay. I understand."

Alyson floated over to the bed and sat down. "Trevor is here, and Mac and Ty are here. You should all go to brunch or something. I'll try to talk to Sophia to see if she'll share anything with me. Check back with me later. In the meantime, go have some fun with our friends."

"Okay. That sounds good. And thanks."

I went downstairs to find Trevor in the kitchen chopping veggies. A quick glance through the glass doors showed Mac and Ty cuddling on the deck, drinking coffee.

"Looks like breakfast," I said as I slid onto a barstool.

"I figured it would be a good day for a big Sunday brunch. We could have gone out, but I found adequate supplies to make a big omelet we can enjoy with the scones I brought. I'm going to fry up some ham too."

"I have fruit; I'll make a fruit salad. And there's champagne and orange juice for mimosas." I opened the refrigerator and began pulling out fruit for the salad.

"I take it things didn't go well with Sophia," Trevor said as I chopped the fruit and he began cracking eggs.

"She won't appear to me. Alyson is going to work on her. In the meantime, I have the whole day free. I'm not sure about Mac and Ty's plans. I'll see if they want to do something."

"Actually, they mentioned something about taking a drive down the coast. I could be wrong, but I had the sense it was a drive of the romantic sort."

"Ah. I should have known."

"I'm off today, if you want to do something. Maybe we can go antiquing or hiking."

I considered the options. "Maybe antiquing. We could have lunch in that cute little town near the antique outlet I've decided I love to poke around in now that you've convinced me that old things are cool."

Trevor poured the beaten eggs into the hot pan. "Sounds like fun. I've been wanting to find a new dresser for my bedroom. The one I have is fine, but it lacks personality. And we still need to find something for you to use as a matting table. The portable table you're using seems functional but lacks pizzazz."

I had to laugh. "Pizzazz?"

Trevor raised a brow and gave it a little wiggle.

"I still can't believe you're the same guy I knew in high school. Trevor Johnson the quarterback would never have used a word like *pizzazz*."

"Trevor Johnson the quarterback grew up."

I smiled. "Yeah. I guess he did at that."

By the time the food was ready, the sun was high in the sky and the morning chill had burned off, so we decided to eat on the back deck. Mac refilled everyone's coffee while Ty made the mimosas and Trevor and I grabbed the food, plates, and utensils. I was looking forward to getting to know Ty a bit better. If he was about to become a significant part of Mac's life, that meant he would become an important part of mine.

Ty didn't know about my unique abilities, and Mac and I had agreed we wanted to take some time before we filled him in, which meant talk of the murders was off the table. Which was just as well. I wanted to focus on other things for a few hours. I asked Ty about his work and he asked about my decision to leave New York. Trevor and Ty had a lively debate about the best surfing beaches in the area, and Mac brought us up to speed on the details of the project she and Ty were working on. By the time we finished the delicious meal Trevor had made for us, we'd covered all the usual topics of conversation. Mac told me that she and Ty planned to take a drive, and I told her Trev and I planned to go antiquing. Antiquing wasn't a hobby Mac and I shared, so I think she was just as happy to have an excuse not to tag along. Ty was heading home after he brought Mac home after their drive, so Trevor and I said our goodbyes in case we missed one another later.

Although we'd taken the dogs for a short walk that morning, I wanted to take them for a longer one before we left for the day, so Trevor and I set off along the bluff trail for the second time that day. The fog that had lingered off the shore had cleared and it looked as if it was going to be a perfect autumn day.

I'd brought along my camera in the event the dolphins we'd seen that morning were still hanging around.

"I heard one of those holiday warehouses opened up about forty miles north of here. If you wouldn't mind, I'd like to stop by while we're out. I think it would be fun to dress up for Halloween."

"I wouldn't mind at all. I was there about a month ago to look for some lights and new Halloween décor for the restaurant. It's pretty awesome. And it's huge. The stock will probably be pretty picked over by now, but it wouldn't hurt to take a look. And we can look at the Christmas stuff while we're there. It might seem too soon, but if you want the best selection, you need to shop early."

I paused and framed a shot of the rolling waves. "I'd like to buy some new decorations for the house. Mom left behind what we had when we returned to New York, so there are a few boxes of lights and bulbs and whatnot, but we never did go all-out in decorating the house. I think I'd like to do that this year. Both the interior and the exterior."

"I'm available to help. I'm really looking forward to the holidays. More so than I have in a long time."

I smiled at Trevor. "Yeah, me too. Let's turn around. It sounds like we have a lot of ground to cover today."

I made sure the animals had plenty of fresh water, and then we set off up the coast. Our first stop would be the holiday warehouse, followed by the antique mall, and then a late lunch. We hadn't seen dolphins on our second walk, but I'd brought my camera with me just in case we caught a glimpse of them during our drive. We were only about ten minutes into our trip when I caught a flash of something out of the corner of my eye.

"Pull over," I said.

Trevor slowed. "Why. What's wrong?"

"Nothing's wrong. I thought I saw something."

Trevor pulled onto the side of the road and stopped.

"There." I pointed to the forest side of the road. I opened the passenger-side door and slipped out.

"An animal?" Trevor asked, getting out of the truck as well.

"No. Not an animal. And not a ghost. It might have been a trick of the light, but I think I saw someone."

Trevor walked around the truck and stood next to me. "It could just be a hiker."

"Maybe. But I have a funny feeling about this. I need to check it out. Do you want to wait here?"

"No, I'm coming with you."

We started slowly toward the spot where I was sure I'd seen a flash of someone moving through the trees. By the time we arrived there, no one was around. I stood perfectly still and turned in a circle. I wasn't sure why I was so certain whom I'd seen—Trevor had made a very good point; there were bound to be hikers out and about at this time of the year. "Avery," I called out. "My name is Amanda. Josie and Sophia told me that you might be in trouble. I'm here to help you."

I waited, but no one appeared.

"You think the flash you saw was the third girl the killer was holding?" Trevor asked.

"I do."

"Why would you think that? We're at least ten miles from the cabin. Besides, it seems there isn't much chance she's still alive."

"Intuition. Now be quiet and wait here. I'm going to try again."

"You know if the flash you saw was Avery, the killer might not be far behind," Trevor warned.

"Good point. Okay, come with me, and keep an eye out, but let me do the talking."

"Are you sure we shouldn't just call Woody?" Trevor took several steps forward as I began to walk slowly toward a large runoff tunnel.

"And tell him what?"

Trevor didn't respond, but he continued to follow me. "Avery, if that was you I saw, I want you to know you can trust me. I can help you. I spoke with Josie and Sophia, and they told me everything. If the man who took you is after you now, he might not be far behind. We need to get you to safety. We need to hurry." I turned and pointed to the truck. "That's our truck. We can take you away from here."

I waited as a small form appeared from the darkness of the drainage pipe. "Is he here?" she asked in a soft voice.

"I don't see him, but we should go right away."

The girl nodded. She continued to make her way out of the pipe toward me.

"This is my friend Trevor," I said. "And I'm Amanda. Let's hurry toward the truck. Once we're safe we can figure out what to do."

The girl looked behind her. "Okay. But we should hurry. I saw him earlier. I don't think he's far away."

Knowing a man with a gun was in the area added enough urgency to the situation that Trevor picked up the girl, whose feet were so bloody she could barely walk, and carried her to the truck. As soon as she was safely in the back seat, we climbed in, turned around, and headed back the way we'd come. Hopefully, the killer hadn't been watching and didn't know we had Avery with us.

"Josie and Sophia are alive?" Avery asked after we'd been on the road for a minute.

"No," I answered. "I'm sorry. They were unable to get away from the man who hunted them."

"But you said you spoke to them," Avery said.

"I did say that, and I did speak to them. I know this will be hard to believe, but I can see and speak to ghosts. I've been helping them figure out what happened to them. They told me about you, so we've been looking for you."

"I see." The girl looked spooked, but she didn't freak out or anything, which was good.

"Should we take her to Woody?" Trevor asked.

"Who's Woody?" Avery asked.

"A friend of mine. He's a cop."

"No!" Avery said with conviction. "No cops."

"I know the man who's chasing you said he was a cop, but Woody isn't like that. He's a good cop. He'll help you."

"No cops," Avery insisted.

I looked at Trevor. "Let's just go back to the house for now. Avery needs medical attention, food, water, and probably sleep. We'll take things one at a time."

"Okay," Trevor agreed.

I turned in my seat so I was looking behind me. "Josie told me the man who killed her hunted her before he shot her, that he gave her a head start. Did the same thing happen to you?"

Avery looked down at her hands. "Yes. That's what happened. He told me he'd give me an hour's head start, and if I could stay alive for seventy-two hours, he'd let me go. I could tell he didn't think I'd be able to survive that long, but I'd almost made it before you found me."

"How long had you been running?" I asked.

"I don't have a way of knowing, but I've been hiding for two nights. We started around noon, I think, and I guess based on the height of the sun it's around noon now, so I should only have had to get through one more day."

"Wow," I was impressed. "You managed to evade this guy for two days?"

"I'm good at hiding. I'm small, and I can fit into small spaces. I could tell he was getting closer, though. I caught sight of him several times since the sun came up this morning. I thought about trying to make it down to the road. I figured maybe I could flag down a car, but I would have had to run through that wide-open meadow to get to the road. I was afraid he'd see me."

Trevor pulled off the highway onto the road leading out to the bluff.

"You're safe now," I said. "When we get to the house we'll clean up your feet and other cuts and get you something to eat. I bet you're hungry."

The girl put her hand on her stomach. "I've been too scared to be hungry."

The poor thing. I bet she was terrified. I had a million questions for her, but first things first. When we got to the house, Trevor carried her in. I made her a bath to soak her feet and other wounds in while he went into the kitchen to make her something to eat. After she soaked in the tub for a bit, I dressed her in a pair of my sweats, then Trevor carried her downstairs, where we treated and wrapped her feet.

"These eggs are really good," the girl said. "I guess I *was* hungry."

"There are more where those came from if you're still hungry," Trevor said.

She looked around the room. "This is a nice house. Do you both live here?"

"I live here," I answered. "Trevor's a friend."

"I see." Avery took another bite of her eggs.

"I'm sure you must be exhausted and would benefit from some sleep. I have just a few questions while you're eating, if that's okay."

Avery shrugged.

"First, what's your last name?"

"Kinkaid."

"Is there someone we can call for you? A friend or family member?"

Avery shook her head. "No. I'm on my own." She looked at Trevor. "Do you have toast?"

Trevor stood up. "Coming right up."

"The other girls were from LA. Are you from LA too?" I asked.

"I'm from a lot of places." The girl looked at me. "I like to move around. But I was taken from LA and brought here. Where is here, anyway?"

"Oregon. Sophia and Josie were picked up by a cop who offered not to arrest them if they agreed to appear in a reality show. Is that what happened to you?"

Avery nodded. "But trust me, I had no idea what the reality show was all about. I figured it would be some sort of *Survivor* thing."

"Do you mind sharing with me the reason you were picked up in the first place?"

She glanced at me with an expression that clearly communicated suspicion. "You a cop?"

"No. And I don't have to share this information with any cops, if that makes you more comfortable. I'm just trying to understand, so I can best help you and Sophia."

The girl narrowed her eyes. "I thought you said Sophia was dead."

"She is. But she refuses to move on until I can answer some questions she has about her life."

"And Josie?"

"She moved on after she was able to understand what had happened to her."

Avery took another bite of her eggs. Trevor put two slices of buttered toast on her plate, then took a seat across the table from her. After a minute or two she spoke. "I like to move around. I live wherever I can find a place to crash and pick pockets to buy food. I'm good and rarely got caught until I was unlucky enough to pick the pocket of a guy who turned out to be an off-duty cop. I didn't want to go to jail, so when he offered me an alternative, I took it." Avery leaned back in her chair and closed her eyes. "I really am tired. Can we take a break?"

"Sure. I'll have Trevor carry you up to my mom's room. She isn't here, but it's all made up. There's an attached bathroom if you need to use it. Before you go, though, I need you to tell me everything you can about the man who tried to kill you."

"Tall. Dark hair and dark eyes. He said his name was Officer Newland when I tried to pick his pocket."

I doubted that was his real name, but it wouldn't hurt to check it out. "Anything else?"

Avery yawned. "He had a scar on his jaw. Right side. Went clear from his ear to his chin."

That could be helpful.

"Oh, and he said he was in the military before he was a cop. At least, that's where he said he got the scar." Avery closed her eyes again. "I really need to sleep."

"Okay. Trev will carry you up and we'll both be here when you wake up. Maybe then we can figure out what to do next."

"No cops."

"No cops," I repeated. "I have a roommate who'll be back later. She's cool, and you can trust her. But other than Mac, we won't tell anyone you're here until we can come up with a plan."

Avery paused. I could sense she wanted to trust us but wasn't quite ready to do it. I supposed after her experience, her distrust was probably stronger than it had ever been. I had a feeling if she was able to leave under her own power she would, but she was obviously exhausted, and her feet were in such bad shape she could barely walk. She had no choice but to stay with us for now.

"Okay," she said. She glanced toward the back door. "Do you think he'll find us?"

"No, I don't think he will." I glanced at Tucker, who hadn't left Avery's side since Trevor had carried her in. "If you'd like, Tucker can sleep with you. He'll provide some extra security."

Avery smiled and ran her hand through his mane. "Okay. I guess I'll feel better with him in the room."

Chapter 6

Monday, October 29

As it turned out, Avery slept right through the rest of the day and the night. While she did, Trevor and I talked about what we should tell Woody. He needed to know Avery had been found and was safe, but we'd promised her no cops. Finally, we decided to tell Woody a half truth: that I had inside knowledge Avery was safe but wasn't at liberty to say anything else just yet. I let him believe my knowledge was supernatural in origin. I figured if he thought my intelligence came from a ghost and not a living being, he'd be less apt to demand a detailed explanation. I also gave him the new description of the killer, including the scar and the name he'd been using. I promised I'd keep digging for details.

Alyson brought the news that Avery was alive to Sophia, which got her to finally reappear to me. I felt

I knew enough about what had happened to the girls that I no longer needed to grill Sophia about her experience. I asked her again if she was ready to move on. Although she felt the pull to do so, she still wanted to wait to pass until she knew her name and more about herself.

The next morning, I helped Avery change her bandages and get dressed while Trevor made her something to eat. Her feet were less painful today, so she was able to limp down to the kitchen with my help.

"So, once the seventy-two-hour mark comes and goes, do you think the psycho cop will give up looking for Avery and take off?" Mac asked as she nibbled on a muffin.

"I don't know," I answered. "I hope so, but I really want to catch this guy. If he leaves the area, that will lessen our chances."

"He'll probably just get another girl," Avery said.

I frowned. "You think he will?"

Avery nodded. "He seemed to have a ritual. I watched as he did the whole thing with the other two girls. My sense was that he needed to have three kills to complete the ritual. I don't think he ever really planned to let me go. I think he just wanted to give me motivation to keep running. It was more fun for him that way."

"So he may keep looking after the seventy-two-hour point," Mac said.

Avery shrugged. "Maybe. I'm not sure, but unless he somehow knows I'm not still in the game, he'll probably keep looking for me, at least for a while."

"We need to tell Woody what's going on," Mac said.

"No cops!" Avery shouted.

"I promised no cops, but we can't know for certain that this crazy guy won't somehow track you here," I said. "We need to get you somewhere safe. Somewhere he'll never find you."

"Do you have somewhere to go?" Trevor asked her.

"I don't have anyone. Like I said, I like to keep moving."

"What about family, even family you haven't seen for a while?" I asked.

"My family is dead. House fire when I was sixteen. The people who said they were there to help me just wanted to send me away to a home. I ran away and I've been on the road ever since."

Avery's story seemed to confirm my suspicion that the killer chose girls he knew wouldn't be missed. "I might have someone who'd let you stay with them while you heal. Someone far away from here."

Avery looked at me, distrust evident on her face. "Who?"

"My mother. She lives in New York. The killer will never find you there."

"The woman whose room I slept in?"

I nodded. "Should I call her?"

Avery hesitated. "Why would your mother want to take care of me? She doesn't even know me."

"She's the sort to help people in need when she can."

"And she's super nice," Trevor added.

"And she has a big house, so there's plenty of room," Mac added.

Avery frowned. "I've never been to New York."

"Why don't I call my mother to make sure she's agreeable, and we can Facetime so you can meet her?"

Avery didn't answer, but I could tell she was thinking it over.

"You'd be safe there," Trevor said.

"What's the catch?" Avery asked.

I glanced at Trevor, who shrugged. I answered, "There is no catch. I'll call my mom and set it up. It would be helpful, though, if you'd agree to talk to our cop friend before you go." I held up a hand. "Just him. He'll come here and talk to you and then, if my mom is agreeable, we'll drive you to the airport and put you on a plane to New York. My mom would pick you up at the airport and take you to her home. You'll be perfectly safe the entire time."

Avery took a deep breath, then blew it out slowly. "Okay. If your mother agrees to your plan, I'll talk to your friend."

As expected, Mom was more than happy to help in any way she could. She arranged for a private jet for Avery from a private-use airport; Avery didn't have ID, so she wouldn't be able to board a commercial jet, but Mom asked a friend who owned a small plane to help out. After I spoke to her, I called Woody and outlined the situation. He agreed to come to the house alone to talk to Avery. I made certain he would agree not to detain her in any way. Woody was a good guy. I had no doubt he wanted to catch the killer as much as we all did, but I also knew he would want to make sure Avery was safe.

I introduced Woody to Avery, and he asked her to tell her story as she remembered it. She began with being caught pickpocketing and then described the offer the off-duty officer made, and how the rest played out. By the time the killer had brought Avery to the house where the girls were held before being brought north, Josie and Sophia were already there. Avery told Woody that she couldn't be certain, but evidence at the house seemed to indicate the three girls who made the trip to Oregon weren't the first ones to have been held there.

Woody asked her for a description of the man who'd tried to kill her. He really wanted a sketch to show around, but Avery refused to have a sketch artist come to the house, so we got my mom on the line and she drew what Avery described. By the time the pair had finished working together and Mom sent it to Woody, we had a good sketch of the killer, and I was confident the girl and my mother would be comfortable with each other.

Woody's lips tightened when Avery said it was her impression that the killer would go in search of another girl now that she'd gotten away. Woody asked Avery if she had any idea where the man might have been staying when we found the cabin. She couldn't offer any ideas, but we all thought that, like the cabin we'd found, it would be somewhere isolated.

Woody gave Avery a burner cell she agreed to carry should he need to contact her. He promised not to tell anyone where she was going. Avery was afraid of cops, especially after what had occurred, and she definitely wasn't comfortable with any of them other than Woody knowing where she was hiding out. I found I had to agree.

Woody left with his notes and sketch, and the rest of us packed a suitcase for Avery with some of Mac's clothes. Avery was a tiny little thing, even smaller than Mac, but they were closer in height than I was. I was sure once Avery settled in with Mom, they'd do some shopping.

"We'll all take you to the airport here," I told Avery later that evening. "When the plane lands, look for Mom. She and a driver will meet you at the gate."

"Your mom has a driver?"

"She has a lot of people working for her. There won't be any need to pick pockets while you're staying with her."

Avery gave me an odd expression. "Aren't you afraid I'll steal from her?"

I looked Avery in the eye. "Will you?"

She shook her head. "Of course not. I owe all of you so much. I can't begin to tell you how grateful I am."

I hugged Avery. "I'm just glad we got to you in time. Have fun with Mom. And let her help you."

Avery picked up the suitcase we'd packed for her. "We should go. I don't think I'll feel safe until I'm away from here."

"I totally understand. Not a lot of people know this, but Mom and I spent two years in witness protection. Not quite the same thing as what you went through, but terrifying all the same."

Avery walked toward my SUV, which we'd decided to take to the airport rather than Trevor's truck. "So your mom will understand if I wake up screaming in the middle of the night?"

"She'll understand, and she'll know how to help. Let her."

******

After the plane took off, we went into town to grab some dinner. Cutter's Cove went all-out when it came to holiday decorations, so we decided to take a walk around the old town section before choosing a restaurant. This part of downtown had broad sidewalks that were lined with cute shops. To the left of the sidewalk, between quaint brick buildings and the street, was a row of trees that were kept neatly trimmed to provide shade but not to be overwhelming. Each year in October they were strung with orange and white twinkle lights. Combined with those lights and the decorations the stores provided, walking here was like being in a real-life Halloween village.

"We never did make it to the Halloween warehouse," I said as I paused in front of a smaller local costume store. "I'm sure there will be much less, but let's pop in to take a look around."

"Fine by me," Trevor said, opening the door to permit Mac and me to enter the quaint little store.

It might not have the warehouse's selection, but it really was festive. "Monster Mash" was playing on the sound system, while large mechanical monsters were set up to greet us as we rounded each corner.

"Do you have the candy you'll need for the trick-or-treaters on Wednesday?" Mac asked Trevor.

"I have plenty of candy, but I could use a few more rubber spiders. The ones I had near the front entry seem to have scampered away."

"Scampered away?" I asked.

"I think they might have been assisted by a group of kids who were in last week."

"Ah," I said, as some boys barreled down the aisle, almost knocking me to the floor. Trevor grabbed my arm, which was probably the only thing that prevented me from ending up on my butt. Didn't those kids have parents?

"I seem to remember you liberating your fair share or rubber spiders when you were a kid," Mac reminded Trevor as we continued down the aisle toward the masks.

"Guilty as charged, which is why I didn't make a big deal of it."

I held up a gruesome mask, considering it. "If we're going out after you close, I don't want to do much to my hair or face, so maybe a mask? I can just wear some jeans and a long-sleeved T-shirt with it."

"A mask would be the easiest," Mac agreed. She looked at Trevor. "What are you dressing up as?"

"Dracula, who is, after all, the sexiest vampire of all." Trevor looked at both Mac and me. "One of you could dress in white and be Dracula's bride. I saw a white wig as we walked in. You might need to wash up before we head out to the bars, but the costume wouldn't require a lot of makeup and you wouldn't need to mess with your hair."

"I think I'll stick to this swamp thing mask," Mac said.

Trevor looked at me. "Amanda?"

I shrugged. "Sure. I'll do it. A white dress and wig and a little makeup to bring out my natural paleness. Seems like an easy costume." I set the mask I had been holding back on the rack. "Let's pay for this stuff and look for a place to eat. Suddenly, I'm starving."

"How about the wharf?" Mac asked. "I hear they decorated the entire wharf and the restaurant at the end is still as good as it ever was."

"Sounds good to me," I said.

Hanging out with Mac and Trevor, doing the same things in the same places we had when we were in high school, was causing a serious case of déjà vu. It was odd, but the nostalgic feelings had both a positive and a negative effect on me. In a way, I felt sad that I had missed so much time with my best friends after Mom and I left Cutter's Cove. But I felt happy I was back now and had plenty of time to make new memories I was sure would last a lifetime. At least, I hoped I did. I couldn't quite get that darn text out of my mind.

To distract myself, I turned my thoughts to Halloweens past. I tried to remember what had become of the photo albums I had created during my two years in Cutter's Cove. Surely I had taken them with me when we left, but for the life of me, I couldn't imagine where they'd ended up. Of course, when we left, Mom and I had planned to come back, so we'd only taken the few things we thought we'd need and left the rest behind. Maybe the albums were still in the closet of my room. When I remodeled it, I'd taken out a wall to add the attached bath, but the closet hadn't been affected. I'd have to look when I got home.

"I think your phone is buzzing," Mac said to me as we walked down the wharf, which had been strung with lights on both sides as well as overhead.

I pulled out my phone from my pocket. "Hey, Woody. What's up?"

"I'm sorry to interrupt your evening, but I have some information you may be interested in."

"Okay. Go ahead."

"The idea that the girls who ended up in Cutter's Cove weren't the killer's first kidnap victims has been on my mind, so I've been looking for unsolved cases that share similar aspects, such as being shot in the back and being found in the wilderness."

"Did you find something?"

"I did. Two years ago this month, two hunters found the body of a young girl in an isolated part of the Cascade Mountains, near Mount Rainer. The girl, initially listed as a Jane Doe, was approximately seventeen years old and died from a gunshot wound to the back. The case was treated as an isolated incident, and the police focused on figuring out who the young woman was so that next of kin could be notified. During the investigation, one of the men assigned spoke to a woman who worked at a minimart off Highway 410. She told him that she remembered seeing a man driving a white panel van with three young women earlier in the month. They had stopped for gas, and the women got out to use the restroom. They stood out in her mind because they were so unkempt. It appeared as if they hadn't had the opportunity to shower, change clothes, or even comb their hair for weeks. When shown the photo of Jane Doe, the clerk couldn't be certain she was one of the girls, but she might have been."

"I don't suppose this guy paid for the gas with a credit card?"

"Cash. And no, he wasn't picked up by the surveillance system."

"Did they ever find the other two girls?" I asked.

"Not at the time, but the remains of two young women were discovered in a remote area the following summer, five miles from each other, by different people. It was suspected the three deaths were related because all the girls were in their late teens and had been shot in the back."

"Was Jane Doe ever identified?"

"The first victim was eventually identified from a missing persons report dated three years earlier. Darlene Woolstone was just fourteen when she ran away from her home in Tacoma. After a bit of digging, it was determined she'd made her way to Seattle, where it was assumed she'd been living right up until she was taken to the mountains and killed."

That seemed to fit the MO in these instances too. Young women who'd run away at an early age and wouldn't be missed by anyone. "And the other two? Were they identified?"

"No. Their remains were badly decomposed and their basic physical characteristics didn't match any missing persons reports. Their identities are still unknown and their killer has never been identified."

I leaned a hip against the railing that separated the wharf from the sea. "So, assuming the man who killed Sophia and Josie is the same one who killed those three young women, it seems there's an identifiable pattern he's compelled to repeat."

"It would seem," Woody said.

"Do you think there might have been others? The three murders you just described took place two years ago. Were there similar murders last year?"

"Maybe. So far, I haven't found any murders with a similar MO that took place last year, but I found some information relating to three murders, all girls between seventeen and twenty, that took place five years ago. This particular set happened near Prince George in British Columbia, but the girls were strangled, not shot, and their bodies were found in seedy motel rooms, not in the forest. Given the differences, it's possible we're looking at a different killer, but my gut tells me all the murders are related. I hate to say it, but I suspect if I look hard enough, I'll find other sets of three murders."

"I think you may be right. Mac, Trevor, and I are in town now, but I'll have Mac see what she can find online when we get back to the house. Even if all the murders didn't take place in this state or even this country, it seems we should be able to figure out more of the pattern. Maybe if we knew when it was first established, it would help us understand who we're dealing with."

Woody sighed. I could hear the fatigue in his voice. "Any little thing would help at this point. Knowing that another girl might be taken as a result of Avery getting away is like waiting for the other shoe to drop."

"I feel the same way. Anything else?"

"I found out the LAPD does not now nor have they ever had a police officer named Newland. Or one with a scar running along his jaw from ear to chin."

"I suspected the killer wasn't a real cop. It'll be harder to find him if he isn't in any systems, but I'm confident something will turn up that will give us the lead we need."

"I hope so."

"Send me everything you have and we'll do what we can. I'll call you later."

"Okay. And thanks. The truth is, we probably wouldn't have discovered the bodies of the girls who were taken this year if not for you."

"They weren't all that isolated. Someone would have found them at some point, though probably not in time to save Avery. I don't know why I can do what I do, but most of the time I'm grateful for the gift."

I filled Mac and Trevor in on what Woody had told me, and we decided to pick up takeout and go back to my house. Mac went up to her room to grab her laptop, while I took the dogs out for a quick bathroom break, and Trevor assembled the plates and cutlery we'd need for dinner. I had a feeling we had a long night ahead of us, but if there was a chance another girl could be taken, we needed to try to get to work right away.

After we ate, and Mac spent some time on the computer, she paused to catch us up. "I haven't found any other murders that took place in sets of three other than the ones we already know about, but that could be because the bodies haven't been found yet. We may need to widen our search to all girls between the ages of sixteen and twenty-two found in remote areas to pick anything up, but that might produce a lot of leads to follow."

"Maybe we can narrow it down a bit more," Trevor said.

"The murders of all three sets of girls we know about took place in October," I said. "That seems significant."

"The set of girls killed longest ago were strangled rather than shot and discovered in motel rooms,"

Trevor said. "I wonder if that means it's unrelated to the second, or if the killer evolved as time went on."

Mac sat back and stared at the screen. She bit her lip as she scrolled through the information she had dug up. "It would help if we could find a similar pattern, either four years ago or last year. I'm going to look for any girls whose bodies were found in remote areas. I have to warn you, this could take a while."

"I'm going to go upstairs to check on Sophia," I said.

"Sunny seems like she needs to go out. I'll take her," Trevor offered.

Mac continued to work, and Trevor and I went our separate ways. I felt our work to catch the killer was the most important thing for us to do, but I still wanted to help Sophia move on. I just wasn't sure how I was going to do that.

"Alyson, Sophia, are you here?" I called out once I entered my bedroom.

"I'm here." Alyson appeared.

"Is Sophia still with you?" I asked.

"She is. We need to find a way to help her move on, even if she doesn't ever find out who she is. I'm afraid we might lose her altogether. I'd hate to see her be one of those spirits destined to wander the void forever."

"I'm just not sure what to do. Unless she can provide new information, I'm not sure we'll ever be able to figure out who she was in life."

Alyson floated over and sat down on the bed. "It does seem as if she was one of the nameless ones who fell through the cracks."

I sat down on the edge of the bed, near where Alyson was lingering. "It seems a little odd to me that she can remember her time in LA but not a single thing before that. Josie remembered swings and grass and was able to build on that. We need to figure out what little tidbit Sophia might be hanging on to."

"I keep thinking about Sissy," Alyson said. "When we asked her to come up with a name, she remembered being called Sissy. Then Josie said she knew her as Sophia, and she agreed to be called that. Maybe Sophia was her street name, or it might have been something she called herself when she was trying to hide from someone. Sissy seems like a real name, or at least a real nickname."

"If that's true, Sissy is most likely a nickname for sister. A big or little sister to someone who called her that as a child."

"Maybe we can find the sister."

"We have Sophia's DNA. Woody didn't find a match in the federal database, but lots of people are having their DNA tested these days. Maybe we can find a familial match."

"It's worth a try," Alyson agreed.

"I saw something on the news recently where they solved a decades-old murder by comparing DNA that was found at the scene but didn't match anyone at the time. Then it wound up matching DNA gathered by one of those ancestry sites that are so popular these days."

"The killer had his DNA tested?"

"No, his cousin did. Once they found the familial match, it was only a matter of time before they were able to track down the guy."

"Totally cool." Alyson began to float around the room.

"I'll call Woody to see about doing that kind of search. I think it might actually work. If we can find a relative, we might be able to get Sophia the answers she needs."

Chapter 7

Tuesday, October 30

When Trevor left and Mac and I went up to bed the night before, we still hadn't found anything relevant or significant, but we'd considered and discarded several possibilities to the specific set of conditions we were looking for. We still didn't know if the three girls who died in British Columbia had been killed by the same monster who killed Sophia and Josie, but we also hadn't found anything that would disprove the theory that they had, other than the difference in method and dump site. Mac planned to continue the search today. I'd also spoken to Woody about looking for a familial match using Sophia's DNA. It was a long shot, but it was all we had.

As I did most mornings, I took the dogs out for a walk. Trevor had joked about coming by with my latte and scone, but I told him that I planned to sleep in, so it would be best if he skipped it. Of course, I had dogs to take out, so sleeping the day away wasn't an option for me anyway.

After walking out to the edge of the bluff, I sat down to give Tucker a rest, while Sunny ran around. Mom had texted me the previous evening to let me know Avery had arrived safely, but I hadn't had a chance to talk to her, so I decided to call.

"Good morning, sweetheart," Mom said. "You have a new number. I didn't even notice it when you called yesterday."

"Good morning to you as well. And yes, I got a new phone. The text you sent last night was forwarded. How are things going?"

"Well. Avery is such a sweet little thing. I'm enjoying her company very much."

"Thanks for helping out. After everything she's been through, she needs a nurturing place to heal."

"Have you found the man who killed the other girls?"

"Not yet, but we're still looking, and so is Woody, of course. Now that we have the sketch you drew from Avery's description, it should be easier to track him down. Especially if he's still around here."

"I know you'll be extra careful until he's caught, but as your mother, I feel it's my duty to remind you."

"I am being careful." I paused to accept a stick from Sunny. I tossed it into the distance, then went on. "I forgot to ask about the show at the gallery last weekend. How did it go?"

"It was very well attended. I was happy with the sales too. I've picked up several new artists recently, and I know they were thrilled with the turnout."

"I'm so happy to hear that."

"I'm looking forward to my visit in December. I've sold most of the seascapes I did the last time I was there and need to restock. I may even come early so I have more time to paint."

"I'd love that. In fact, why don't you just come for Thanksgiving and stay through New Year's?"

"I'd enjoy that. Let me think about it a bit and I'll let you know for certain what my plans are."

I hated to worry my mom, but I knew it was past time for me to tell her about the text. I owed her the truth. "Before we sign off, there's something else," I said.

"Sounds serious."

"It's not. At least, I don't think it is. I hesitate even to bring it up, but we've always had an open and honest relationship, and I don't want to alter that at this point."

"I'm listening."

"I received a text last week. It was a photo of the Bonatello brothers with a few words written beneath it. I haven't received anything else, and I called Donovan right away."

I could hear Mom breathing, but it took a minute for her to respond. "I see. And what did Donovan say?"

"That there's been some activity in the Bonatello family. Several high-ranking members were killed, including Franco, the father. Vito Bonatello is the new leader of the family. He's Clay's son. At first, Donovan thought he might have been the one to send the message, but he's since learned he was detained for questioning at the time the text was sent. Donovan had someone from the Portland marshal's office come get my phone so they can monitor it. That's why I have a new number."

"And does Donovan think you're in danger?"

"Actually, no. Not at this point. I still had the same cell number I had in New York, and it's Donovan's opinion that whoever sent the text might not even know I'm not there. Whoever's monitoring my phone is forwarding all my texts, and I have access to my old voice mailbox. Donovan assured me that he's looking into things, and he cautioned me not to freak out, so I'm working hard to stay calm and stay focused on the things in my life I have at least a small amount of control over."

"I think that's a good idea. And I want to thank you for explaining what's happened. If you won't consider it to be interfering, I think I'd like to call Donovan and speak to him directly."

"Of course I don't mind. We've always been in this together, and it affects you almost as much as it affects me. Just try not to worry. If there's one thing I learned the last time, it's that if you let fear consume you, it eats away at your life."

"I agree. And I'm so proud to have raised such a strong, wise daughter. I'll check in with Donovan, but I'll try not to obsess."

"You and me both."

Mom and I spoke for a while longer before I hung up and headed back to the house. Mac was probably up, and I wanted to go over some thoughts I'd had regarding the man I suspected was still out there waiting for the opportunity to complete his third kill of the year.

Mac was sitting at the kitchen table with her laptop when the dogs and I arrived. I poured myself a cup of coffee and sat down across from her.

"I think I found something," she said.

"What?"

"The remains of a woman named Tina Osborn were found in the Pasayten Wilderness up near the Canadian border three summers ago. It appeared she'd been dead for six months to a year by then, which means she most likely died the previous summer or fall; it was unlikely she was dumped at that elevation after the snow fell. According to what I could find, she'd been shot in the back. I haven't been able to find reports of other similar deaths, so I don't know for certain this fits our killer, but given where the body was found, it seems reasonable to me there could have been three deaths and the remains of the other two bodies were simply never found."

"The remote location and the fact that she was shot in the back does seem to fit. I really want to catch this guy."

Mac sighed. "Yeah. The idea that this guy could be responsible for more than a dozen deaths makes me sick to my stomach." Mac leaned back in her chair. "We have a description now, with the sketch your mom helped Avery with. If the guy is still in this area, it seems to me that someone would have seen him. Do you know if Woody is showing the sketch around?"

"I'm not sure. I'm assuming he must be, though he might not want the guy to know we're on to him. If he knows we have a sketch, you'd think he'd move on. His staying around here is our best chance of catching him. I'm going to scramble an egg. Do you want one?"

"Yeah, I guess I'm hungry," Mac answered.

"I spoke to my mom," I said. "She said Avery's doing well."

"That's good. The poor thing. She went through so much."

"She really did, but Mom will spoil her, which should help."

"Did you tell your mom about the other matter?" Mac asked.

"I did. I could tell she's worried, and I hated to do that, but she has a right to know what's going on. Mom's a strong woman, and a text is nothing like the flat-out threat we lived with last time. I think she'll deal with things okay." I pulled out my new phone and looked at it. "I need to let a few people like Caleb and Chelsea know I have a new number so whoever's watching my old phone doesn't have to keep forwarding everything to me."

"That would probably be a good idea."

After we ate, Mac returned to her research and I decided to go into town. We were just about out of kitchen staples such as eggs, milk, and bread. I wasn't sure why I hadn't made more of an effort to cook since Mom left. I enjoyed cooking, and most days I had the time. I guess it was easier to make a sandwich or grab some takeout, but now that winter was just around the corner, it would be nice to have some homemade soups or casseroles to enjoy while we watched the storms roll in.

As long as I was in town, I'd fill my tank and get my SUV washed. After that, I'd hit the cleaners, the bakery, and then the market. It was while I was pumping gas that I saw a man doing the same in the next aisle. He was driving a blue truck with a camper shell, which wasn't unusual, but I couldn't help but notice that despite the day being fairly warm, he had the hood of his sweatshirt pulled up over his head, concealing much of his face. Again, there were guys who wore hoodies 365 days a year regardless of the weather, but this man stood out to me.

I tried not to stare at him as he finished pumping his gas and went inside. Ending my own fill-up session with my tank not yet finished, I followed him. He headed into the men's room, so I feigned an interest in the candy selection while I waited for him to come out. I wished I could get a better look at his face. Between the hoodie and the dark glasses he wore, it was hard to get a good look at his features, but my gut told me this might very well be the killer.

As he came out of the men's room and walked to his truck, I returned to my SUV and decided to follow when he pulled away. "Call Woody," I said aloud.

"Calling Woody," Siri responded.

After three rings, Woody picked up. "Hey, Amanda. I was just about to call you."

"I think I might have spotted the killer."

My words were met with silence.

"Did you hear me?"

"Yes. Where are you?" Woody asked.

"On Highway 28. I'm following a blue Dodge truck with a white camper shell. The license number is 358WOT. I don't know for sure the guy I'm following is the killer. He has on dark glasses and a hoodie, so I didn't get a good look at his face, but my gut is telling me to follow him, so I am."

"Whatever you do, I don't want you to engage the guy in any way."

"I won't. I'm hanging back. He probably doesn't even know I'm following him. I just want to see where he goes."

"If he pulls off the road, hang back farther. If this man is the killer, he's probably very aware of his surroundings. If you're following him even from a distance, he most likely knows."

"Yeah. I'll be careful. I just want to see where he's going. Hang on, he's getting off the highway. He just pulled on to Highway 53 south. I'm following."

"If you do, he'll definitely see you."

"If he's kidnapped another girl, we need to find out where he's staying. If it makes you more comfortable, you can stay on the line with me."

"I'm definitely staying on the line and I'm heading in your direction."

"If you head south on 101 you'll probably intercept us. I have a feeling he's taking the long way around to the same area where we found the cabin that was used to hide the three girls. There are a lot of dirt roads with rustic cabins in that area."

"Maybe you should abort. I don't want you getting hurt."

"If he's the one, he's killed a whole lot of girls. As long as I have my eyes on him, I'm going to follow."

"But…"

"He just pulled onto a side road. I'm going to send you my GPS location; the service is going to get dicey and I may lose you."

"Following him is much too dangerous. I'm telling you to hang back."

I decided not to answer. There was no way I was going to lose this guy. If Woody wanted me to be safe, he needed to hightail it up here and take over from me.

When the truck turned onto a dirt road, I pulled over. He'd see me for sure if I tried to follow now. I still had a line indicating spotty service, so I sent Woody my updated GPS location. Given that the guy had taken the long way around, it shouldn't take Woody all that long to come in from the south.

I knew I should wait, and I did for a while, but eventually my curiosity got the better of me and I got out of my car and headed down the dirt road on foot. The cabin was only about a quarter mile away. The blue truck was parked in front of it. I wasn't dumb enough to actually approach the cabin, and it looked as if there was only one road in and out, so I turned to return to my car. It was then I saw the front door open. The man I had seen at the gas station stepped out, only this time he was dressed in fatigues and without a hoodie. He carried a rifle in one hand and a rope tied around the waist of a girl who looked no older than fifteen in the other.

I put a hand over my mouth to prevent the gasp I suspected was just waiting to escape. *Come on, Woody. Get here.*

The man set off on foot into the forest, pulling the girl behind him. I decided to follow. I knew it was risky, but he could easily disappear in the dense brush and I didn't want to lose him. I just hoped Woody would be able to find me when he got here. It occurred to me that this was the perfect time for a Baggie full of bread crumbs to leave a trail.

I hung back as far as I could so as not to be seen, but not so far that I thought I'd lose him. If he followed his usual pattern, he'd let the girl go and give her a head start. I wasn't sure what he would do once the clock was started, but I hoped he'd just wait, or even return to the cabin, giving Woody time to catch up.

We'd been walking for about twenty minutes when he stopped. I watched as he untied the girl, then said something to her. The poor thing looked terrified. After a few minutes, she took off running. I wanted to follow her but knew I needed to keep my eyes on him. I really hoped he'd return to the cabin, but instead he just stood there and stared into the distance. I supposed he was looking for signs of where she'd gone. The terrain was hilly, and depending on the direction she took, she could very well become visible once she reached the ridge.

I'm not sure how long I waited while he watched the ridge. Maybe twenty minutes. Maybe more. I felt my stomach knot with tension as I realized the girl might very well give her location away if she wasn't smart about the direction she chose. I took a step toward the clearing to get a better view. The movement must have caught the guy's eye because the next thing I knew, he was looking directly at me.

"Well, well, well. What do we have here?"

I didn't say anything. I mean, really, what was there to say?

The guy raised his gun and pointed it directly at me. "Run."

I did as he instructed, acting on instinct more than anything else. I tried to zigzag as I made my way through the forest. My inclination toward survival wouldn't allow me to stop, even though I knew it was only a matter of time before a bullet pierced my flesh, ending my life.

I heard the shot a split second before I dove for cover. I expected that would be the last thing I would ever do, so I was surprised to find I was very much alive when I hit the dirt. I stayed perfectly still. Had he missed?

I was frozen with indecision. Should I get up and try to run? Should I stay where I was? Should I just pray? It was in that moment I heard running feet. I sat up and turned around to find Woody coming toward me.

"Woody?" I cried as shock set in and my body started to shake.

"Are you okay?" He knelt beside me. He pulled me into his arms. I began to sob uncontrollably.

"The killer," I gasped between sobs.

"Dead."

"The girl?"

Woody looked around. "I need to look for her. Are you okay?"

I nodded. "I'm fine." I stood up. My legs were still shaky, but I knew I was all right. "What happened?"

"I came over that little ridge just in time to see him point his gun at your back. I somehow managed to get off a shot before he did. I'm still not sure how that happened."

I took several deep breaths, willing my heart to slow. "We need to find the girl. She had maybe a thirty-minute head start."

"We'll find her."

I nodded and started walking. Woody took my arm and helped me over a fallen log. My legs were still shaky but getting steadier.

"Any idea where she was heading?" Woody asked.

I pointed. "She took off in that direction. I was waiting for her to show up on the trail as she climbed up onto the ridge, but she never did. She must have gone into the water and crossed the river."

"That was smart," Woody said.

"It was. It'll be hard to find her before dark."

"If she crossed the river, we have an area to search. I'll call in the chopper."

It took hours to find the girl, even though a chopper and twenty search-and-rescue workers showed up to look for her. She must have been well versed in the terrain, and she was very motivated to stay hidden. She had cuts and bruises on her legs, arms, and torso when we found her, but otherwise she was fine. Terrified, but fine. Unlike the other girls, Samantha was from nearby and had a family who was worried about her, so there was a teary reunion when she and her parents were finally reunited.

******

Later that evening, I sat with Mac and Trevor under the stars. It was chilly, but he had built a fire in the pit and we were all wrapped up in blankets. I'd decided not to fill my friends in on all the facts relating to the death of the man who'd killed the two young girls because I didn't want to give them a heart attack, so Woody and I worked out a story that allowed us to let Mac, Trevor, and Mom know what had happened, but not how close I had come to dying too. I figured everyone was already worried enough about me after the text I'd received.

It had definitely been a harrowing day, and not one I'd ever care to repeat, but it was a huge relief to know that the man who had killed Josie and Sophia would never hurt another girl. The one negative aspect to his being dead was that he'd never answer the questions we still had, like why he had done what he had and where were the bodies of any other women he'd killed. Woody promised to keep looking for other deaths that might be linked to him, but I doubted we'd ever have all our answers.

"Now, if we can just find Sophia her answers, we'll be able to put this whole thing behind us," Trevor said as he stirred the fire.

"I'm working on a couple of things," Mac said. "Ty is helping. I don't want to sound overly optimistic, but I have a good feeling about the direction in which we're heading. I take it Woody didn't find anything by looking for familial DNA?"

"He's still looking, but there's a lot of data to go through. Even if the DNA search works as we hope it will, it might take a very long time."

"I guess it was always a bit of a long shot," Mac admitted.

"I've been thinking about the fact that Sophia has begun to remember things from her time in LA and, of course, after being taken by the madman who killed her, yet she still hasn't remembered a single thing from her life before," I said.

"What about it?" Mac asked.

"What if the reason she has no memories of her life before LA is because she had no memories of her life before LA?"

"Huh?" Mac looked totally confused.

"What if Sophia had amnesia before she was kidnapped?"

"That could account for her being on the streets in the first place," Trevor offered.

"Exactly," I said. "What if Sophia was in LA for a reason other than running away when she had an accident? Maybe she was mugged or hit by a car. What if she couldn't remember who she was or why she was there, so she ended up wandering the streets dazed and confused?"

Trevor frowned. "Why wouldn't she get help? Go to the cops?"

"Maybe she did," I said.

Mac's eyes got big. "You think Sophia was injured in an accident that caused her to forget who she was, or possibly even where she was, so she went to a policeman for help, and this particular policeman, who wasn't even a real policeman, took advantage of her state of confusion and kidnapped her."

"It's a theory."

"Yeah, but what are the odds that Sophia would happen to go to this particular cop?" Trevor asked.

"We suspect he trolled for his victims among the homeless. If Sophia was dazed and confused, she could have ended up with a particular group of people. A lot of the homeless suffer from mental health issues. Sophia might have appeared to fit right in."

"So we need to look for someone who might have received medical treatment for a head injury," Mac said.

"If she received medical treatment, wouldn't they know at the hospital that her head trauma was severe?" Trevor asked.

"Maybe. But she might not have developed symptoms until later," I answered.

"It seems equally likely that she never sought out medical help," Mac stated. "Still, it wouldn't hurt to look. I wonder if the autopsy showed signs of head trauma."

"I'll call Woody to ask him."

"It's late," Trevor reminded me. "You might want to wait until the morning."

"Yeah, it can wait." I reached my arms over my head. "I think I'm going to take the dogs out for a quick bathroom break and then go up to bed."

"I'll come out with you and then head home," Trevor offered. He got up and kissed Mac on the cheek. "I'll see you tomorrow."

Trevor took my hand in his as we walked through the house and then stepped out onto the porch leading to the drive. "Are you going to be okay?" he asked.

"I am. It's been a long day, but I'm sure I'll be right as rain once I get some sleep."

"I hope so."

"And I'm looking forward to the trick-or-treating thing tomorrow. Do you need help setting up?"

"I don't have a lot to do. It starts at four o'clock and runs until nine. If you and Mac want to come by at about three thirty, that would be great. And remember to bring something to change into so we can go out afterward."

"I'll bring something to wear, but I can't guarantee I'll have the energy to go barhopping after handing out candy for five hours."

Trevor put his arm around my shoulders and pulled me toward his side. "If not, then we can go back to my place and have a quiet Halloween with a bottle of wine."

"That," I said, resting my head on his shoulder, "sounds great."

Chapter 8

Wednesday, October 31

I really did plan to sleep late, but as with many well-laid plans, that wasn't how things turned out. It wasn't even light yet when I found myself crawling out of bed after suffering a restless night. It had been a while since I'd had such severe nightmares, but after almost losing my life, I supposed a delayed reaction of some sort was to be expected.

Pulling on sweatpants and a heavy sweatshirt, I headed out with the dogs. I decided to bring my camera because I was out early enough to catch the sunrise. As many times as I'd photographed the sunrise from my house by the sea, the intensity of the colors never ceased to amaze me. The clouds that had rolled in overnight were beginning to clear, which I hoped would mean an even more brilliant sunrise than usual.

Despite the fact that I'd gotten almost no sleep the night before, I found I was still very much looking forward to the day ahead. I'd always enjoyed Halloween. I loved the dressing up, the decorations, even the occasional horror movie marathon. I knew Mac had some of the old classics on DVD. Maybe if we did decide to skip the barhopping, we could watch *The Blob* or *The Creature from the Black Lagoon* while we shared that bottle of wine. Of course, after the very real horror movies that had played over and over in my mind for half the night, maybe we should stick with *It's the Great Pumpkin, Charlie Brown.*

As the sky began to lighten, I let my mind wander back to the Halloweens I'd spent in Cutter's Cove as a teen. The Haunted Hayride was a blast, and I still remembered the very real ghost mystery I'd solved my first year in town. I sometimes wondered what had happened to some of the friends Mac, Trevor, and I had had back then. I'd have to ask them. There was a good chance one or both of them had stayed in contact with some of the old crowd.

I took out my camera and began snapping shots as the sky turned to red. The reflection of the clouds on the water was going to produce some truly exceptional photos. I angled my lens a bit to the left and then a bit to the right. I took several photos with the lens zoomed in and then zoomed it out. Somewhere in the midst of capturing what had to amount to at least a hundred photos of the sunrise, I caught a photo of Sunny and Tucker playing tug-of-war with a large stick, and that was the photo I most wanted to process, mat, and hang on my wall.

I hadn't heard from Donovan, but I hadn't been quite as able to forget about the text as I'd been telling everyone I had. I decided to call him before starting what I was sure would be a busy day.

"Any word?" I asked.

"Not a one. The tech guys were able to trace the text back to an origin point right here in New York. We still don't know who sent it, but there haven't been any additional texts to your phone and I haven't heard your name mentioned in any of the conversations we're monitoring."

"But you'll continue to monitor? Just in case?"

"We will. And I think you should continue to be aware of your surroundings. Sometimes these things don't play out right away."

"I know. And I'll keep my head up. Did my mom call?"

"She did." Donovan's voice softened. "I was happy to hear from her. It's been a long time. It was good to catch up."

I always suspected Donovan had a thing for my mom. Not that he could or would act on it. But he sure did seem happy to have spoken to her. "You know, you aren't my handler anymore. I don't think it would be inappropriate to call Mom every now and then. Maybe meet for lunch. She's in New York most of the time."

"I really did enjoy our chat. We ended up talking for almost two hours. I might just call her to check in with her again."

By the time the dogs and I returned to the house, Mac was awake. I poured myself a cup of coffee and joined her on the back deck.

"Beautiful sunrise," she said.

"It was exceptional," I agreed. "That burst of purple toward the middle took my breath away."

"Too bad your mom wasn't here. She loves watching the sun rise."

"I took a bunch of photos. I might send her a few. And she's thinking of extending her stay from before Thanksgiving until after New Year's."

"That's great. I miss her when she isn't here, which is odd because I don't really miss my own mother. Does that make me a horrible daughter?"

"Not horrible. Pretty normal. Your mom is great, but I don't remember the two of you being particularly close."

"We weren't. She didn't get the whole math and science thing. And she used to yell at me to get off my computer, like I was wasting my time on video games or something. I think she has a lot more in common with my siblings than with me, but we still enjoy spending time together as long as the time we spend is brief. I want to be here for Christmas, but I'm thinking about visiting the family for a week or two in January, when the pressure of the holidays isn't a factor."

"I remember your mom liked to go all-out for the holidays."

"She still does. Her house is like Santa's Village. I know some people find that charming, but I think it's a bit much. Not that I have anything against a tree and a few lights, but a Santa toilet seat that says ho, ho, ho, when you sit down is just a tad over the top."

I laughed out loud. "Are you serious? Does she actually have a talking seat?"

"She does. And she has a mechanical Santa that plays Christmas carols twenty-four-seven, and don't get me started on the reindeer poop in the bathroom."

"Reindeer poop?"

"It's soap, but it looks like poop."

Yikes.

"Don't get me wrong. I love my mom, and I guess growing up I enjoyed the effort, but somewhere along the way I began to find it cloying. The last time I spent Christmas with Mom, we had a huge fight, so I've tried to avoid visiting at that time of year ever since."

"Well, Mom and I will be happy to have you here, and I don't plan on buying a talking Santa toilet seat, though the reindeer poop sounds like fun."

Mac rolled her eyes.

"I already talked to Trev, and he'll be spending the holidays with us. He closes for three days for Christmas, and of course Thanksgiving Day. You're welcome to invite Ty if you'd like."

"Maybe," Mac answered. "It would be fun for all of us to go to the Christmas Carnival again. Chelsea mentioned they still do the Christmas play, and the rides and games are always fun. I might even offer to help out this year, as long as no costumes of any kind are involved."

"Aw, you made a cute elf."

"It was humiliating."

"I don't know. I seem to remember us all having a lot of fun. I can't wait. It's going to be just like old times."

Mac stood up and picked up her coffee cup. "Yeah. It'll be fun to relive a few of our old traditions. I'm going in. I want to call Ty, then spend a few hours on the computer before we have to get ready for trick-or-treat."

"I'll probably be in soon too. I'm excited to help out at the restaurant."

"Me too. I used to love trick-or-treating as a kid."

******

Later that morning, I heard Mac let out a little squeal. I hurried down the stairs to find out what all the excitement was about.

"Ty found Sophia, only her name isn't Sophia. It's Cicely. Cicely Anderson."

"Really?" I hurried over to Mac's side. On the screen was a photo of a woman who definitely looked like the ghost we knew as Sophia. "Who is she?"

"She was a wannabe actress who moved to LA five months ago from Kansas. Ty tracked down her agent, who told him that she'd done a few commercials, then disappeared. The agent said Cicely, who everyone called Sissy, had been homesick, so she wasn't really surprised when she didn't show up for an audition she had lined up. She assumed she'd decided to throw in the towel and go home."

"When was that?"

"Three weeks ago."

"I wonder what happened three weeks ago."

"Ty, genius that he is, did some digging and found a police report about a hit and run. Apparently, the victim, a young woman who told onlookers she was on her way to an audition, had been hit by a car while running across the street to catch a bus. She didn't seem hurt and refused medical attention, even though she'd hit her head, so the cop who responded let her leave after she insisted she absolutely couldn't miss the very important audition her agent had lined up."

"So I guess we can assume that at some point after the cop let her go, but before she made it to the audition, she became confused and disoriented."

"That would be my guess. There's no way to know, unless she remembers, how long she wandered around before the fake cop picked her up, but it seems the story fits."

"I guess we should tell her," I said. "Maybe once we get her started, she'll remember the rest."

"I think we have enough to at least try," Mac agreed.

I nodded. "Alyson," I called.

"What's up?" she asked when she appeared.

"Is Sophia with you?"

"She's around. Why?"

"I think we found out who she was. Can you ask her to come talk to us?"

Alyson nodded. "Yeah. Hang on."

"Alyson went to get her," I told Mac.

"I figured, based on your end of the conversation. I wish I could see her."

"Yeah. Me too. Although once we help Sophia move on, I have the feeling Alyson will merge inside me."

"That must be so weird, having part of yourself popping in and out like that."

"Very weird," I confirmed.

"Okay. We're here," Alyson said.

I smiled at Sophia. "I think we have your answers. Mac," I nodded toward her as she sat quietly, listening to my side of the conversation, "found out your name was Cicely Anderson. You moved to LA from Kansas five months ago to pursue a career as an actress."

"Sissy," the girl whispered. "I remember. My parents are dead, but I have a sister, Beatrice."

"We'll track Beatrice down and let her know what happened."

"She's going to be so upset. She never wanted me to go to LA. She said it was too dangerous. I guess she was right."

I glanced at Mac. "We believe, based on the information we found, that you were hit by a car on your way to an audition three weeks ago. You hit your head, but you refused medical attention. You never made it to the audition, so we assume you might have become confused. You might even have suffered some sort of amnesia."

Sissy looked confused. "Yes. That part is still fuzzy. I do remember Kansas, and I have a few images of LA, but I don't remember what happened that caused me to end up with the man who killed me. I guess it might come back over time."

"I guess it might."

"Is that enough?" Alyson asked. "Are you ready to move on?"

Sissy nodded. "I think it's time. Maybe my parents will be waiting for me on the other side."

"I'd like to think they will be," I said.

"Can you tell Bea that I'm okay? Tell her that I missed her after I left for LA. Tell her that I slept with Gordo every night."

"Gordo?" I asked.

"She'll know. Just tell her."

"Okay," I agreed. "I'll tell her after she's been officially notified by law enforcement of your passing."

Alyson held out her hand. Sissy took it. She turned and looked at me one last time. "Thank you. I'm sorry about what happened, but I want you to know I appreciate everything you did to help me find my answers."

"I was happy to. I guess in a way it's sort of my job."

******

"Oh my gosh, did you see that little girl dressed like a frog?" I said to Mac later that evening after things had begun to wind down.

"Talk about adorable. Those huge brown eyes staring back from the green headpiece made me want to pick her up and give her a great big hug."

"And those two little boys with the curly blond hair and huge blue eyes that were dressed as sheep. I don't usually spend a lot of time daydreaming about being a parent, but all these cute kids are seriously messing with my biological clock."

Mac laughed. "Careful, Amanda. I hear once that clock gets started, it has a way of running away with you."

"Don't worry. While these kids are pulling at my heartstrings, bearing and raising children is the last thing on my mind right now. I figure I still need to find my Prince Charming to whisk me away to the lovely pink castle on the top of the magical hill in an enchanted land filled with unicorns before I decide to take the plunge."

Mac opened a mini Snickers and popped it in her mouth. "I know you're kidding, but you never know when Prince Charming is waiting in the wings to make his move. The pink castle I could do without, but the unicorns sound like fun."

"So things are going well with Ty?" I asked, even though I'd promised myself I wouldn't.

Mac blushed. "You have no idea. He's... well, he's just so great. To be honest, that sort of scares me."

"Scares you?"

"It's all so new. Everything feels fragile, but I'm so in to him. I'm afraid that what I feel isn't real or, even worse, that he doesn't feel about me the way I feel about him."

I smiled as I glanced out the window. "I think he might feel exactly about you the way you do about him."

"Why do you say that?"

"Look outside."

Mac looked out the window and her mouth fell open. Ty, dressed in a black tux that perfectly accented vampire fangs, had shown up in a horse-drawn carriage with jack-o'-lanterns hanging from the front. "He said he had to work," Mac gasped.

"Oh, I think this grand, romantic gesture was plenty of work."

Mac stood gaping at the man who had just hopped down from the carriage.

I couldn't help but grin. "It looks like your ride has arrived, Cinderella. Have fun, but watch out for those pesky unicorns."

******

"You got a new chair," I said as I walked out onto Trevor's deck and found a lounge chair built for two.

"I saw it online and figured it might come in handy on those cold nights when cuddling makes sense. It's supposed to be a chair for two, but I'm sure you and Mac and I can all fit."

"I love it," I said as I settled onto one side. Trevor tossed a blanket over my legs, then headed over to toss a match on the fire he'd already built in the pit. "There's even a holder for your wine."

"One on each side. I guess if the three of us do share the chair, I'll have to rig something up for the third glass."

Trevor topped off my wine, then climbed into the chair next to me. I wrapped the blanket around the two of us. "I've missed this," I said as I laid my head on Trev's shoulder. "All those beach parties where the three of us would wrap ourselves up in a blanket and talk the night away while the waves crashed in the distance. Of course, I'll admit this deck overlooking the waves combined with your fancy new chair is a bit of an upgrade."

"And let's not forget the wine," Trev added.

"The wine is delicious. And while I'm happy Ty showed up to whisk Mac away, I'm sorry she isn't here with us."

"Yeah, me too. The three of us can do a movie night later in the week, or even over the weekend. Maybe Sunday."

"That would be fun. Although I'm not sure I'm in the mood for a horror fest this year."

Trevor wound the fingers of his left hand through my right. "There's been enough horror in our lives this past week. I'm really glad you got to that girl in time, but the fact that you put yourself in danger sort of terrifies me."

"I didn't intend to put myself in danger. I just wanted to be sure the killer didn't get away, and I guess I might not have taken the time to think things through. No need to lecture me, though. Woody already took care of that."

"You can't blame him. I bet you took ten years off the guy's life."

Trevor was right. I'm sure he missed a few heartbeats when he saw the killer's gun trained on me.

"I guess I do tend to be something of a danger magnet," I admitted. "Which is odd, because I'm not particularly brave."

"I have to disagree with that one. You're the bravest woman I've ever met. You seem to have the capacity to take whatever life throws at you without even breaking a sweat."

"Oh, I broke a sweat when I realized he intended to shoot me," I countered.

"Maybe. But you still put your life on the line to follow him. You put the well-being of that girl above your own. There aren't a lot of people who would have done that."

I let out a slow breath and willed my body to relax. "I'm sure that isn't true. I'm sure most people would have followed him. Although most people would probably have done a better job of staying hidden. I need to work on my stalking skills."

"Lessons from a cat."

I turned my head slightly. "Huh?"

"Stalking your prey is a lesson you should take from a cat."

I grinned. "True. Speaking of lessons, when do you want to start your dance lessons?"

"Anytime is fine."

"How about now?" I suggested.

"Now?"

I tossed back the blanket and stood up. "Sure. Why not. There's plenty of space out here."

"But we don't have music."

"That's okay." I held out my hand. "I'll hum."

Trevor shrugged. "Okay. If that's what you want to do."

I took Trevor's hands in mine, then pulled him to his feet and into my arms. "Now just follow my lead."

Trevor brushed his lips against my neck. "Anywhere, anytime."

Up Next From
Kathi Daley Books

Preview

Friday, November 16

"Morning, Hap," I said to Hap Hollister as my dog Tilly and I entered his home and hardware store to deliver his mail.

"Mornin', Tess; Tilly. Are you all set for your trip?"

I nodded. "We are. When my mom first suggested that we head up to Timberland Lake for Thanksgiving, I wasn't sure that was what I wanted to do. But Mom seems to really want to go, and with Aunt Ruthie at Johnny's for the holiday, they decided to close the restaurant from this Sunday until the Monday after Thanksgiving. It seemed like a good opportunity, and I hated to have her waste her time off."

Hap ran a hand through his thick white hair. "Sounds like it might be fun. Is Tony going with you?"

"He is. I have an adoption clinic tomorrow, and Mom and Aunt Ruthie plan to be open as well, so we're all heading out on Sunday morning."

"Mike going as well?" Hap asked as he began to sort through the stack of mail I'd left on his counter.

"Actually, he is. He got Frank to cover for him, so he has the whole week off." My brother, Mike Thomas, is a police officer right here in White Eagle, Montana, and Frank Hudson is his partner. "Bree is closing the bookstore and coming with us, so I imagine we'll have a nice time. Are you going to Hattie's for the holiday?" Hattie Johnson was Hap's wife, or ex-wife, or something. I wasn't exactly sure about the details. What I did know was that they used to be married and lived together and now they didn't live together, but they did date.

"Yup. Hattie's planning a traditional meal with all the fixin's. Should have enough leftovers to last several days at least."

"That's what I love about Thanksgiving. All the leftovers. Do you have any outgoing mail?"

Hap nodded. "Hang on, I'll get it."

I walked over to Hap's woodburning stove to warm up while I waited. We'd had a cold November so far, as well as several snow showers. I had to admit I had a few reservations about heading up to Timberland Lake despite what I'd said to Hap. Not that I wasn't looking forward to cuddling up by the fire with my boyfriend, Tony Marconi, but Timberland Lake was the same place where my dad went fishing alone every fall, and I had to wonder why, out of all the possible vacation spots, my mom had picked that specific one to have our family holiday. To be honest, ever since I found out my dad was most likely not dead, as we'd all believed for years, I'd been questioning a lot of things.

"Here you go." Hap handed me a stack of mail. "I'm going to miss your sunny face next week, but I hope you have a wonderful time."

"Thanks, Hap. And I hope you and Hattie have a wonderful holiday as well."

After Tilly and I left Hap's store, we continued down the street, dropping off mail and pausing to chat with the people we met along the way. I really love my job. Not that I'd lay awake at night when I was a child dreaming of life as a mail carrier for the US Postal Service, but delivering the daily mail to the merchants in White Eagle gave me the opportunity to stay current with the local news *and* the local gossip.

Not that I couldn't have stayed up-to-date by hanging out in the restaurant my mom owned and operated with my Aunt Ruthie, but there was something pretty perfect about being outdoors in the fresh air for most of the day. I glanced up at the dark clouds overhead. Well, at least it was usually nice to be outdoors. I had to admit that when the cold Montana winter took hold, there were days I found myself wishing I'd been a hairdresser, a florist, or even a podiatrist.

"Morning, Bree," I greeted my best friend, Bree Price, who also happened to be Mike's girlfriend. "The store looks fantastic."

"Thanks. I figured the Christmas rush will have started by the time we return from our trip, so I wanted to have all the decorating taken care of before I left."

"I love the little Victorian village. It's so quaint and perfect. Very bookish."

Bree smiled. "Thanks. I like it. I got the idea from your mom. The Santa's Village she sets up in the restaurant every year is adorable. I wanted to do something similar yet smaller, with a Dickens feel. I'm also going to put a tree in the corner I cleared out near the front door. I want a fresh tree, not a fake, so I figured I'd cut one down while we're up at the lake. When people ask where I got it, I'll have a story to go with the tree."

"I'm pretty sure Tony is bringing his truck, although we do have two dogs and two cats to transport. Let's make sure Mike brings his truck too. He has a back seat, so you can bring Mom with you. We'll have cat carriers on our back seat."

Bree continued to hang the white twinkle lights she'd been stringing around the store when I walked in. "I'm excited about the trip. I've never been to Timberland Lake, but I hear it's beautiful."

"I've never been either," I answered. "In fact, I don't think any of us have, so it'll be a new experience all around."

"I wonder why your mom chose that specific lake if she'd never been there," Bree mused.

"My dad used to go up there every year. I guess he must have told her about it."

Bree's smile faded. "Maybe she's missing him."

I paused. "Maybe. Although he's been gone for a long time. I have a feeling there's something else behind her desire to rent a cabin at that lake, although I have no idea what it is."

Bree shrugged. "I don't suppose it really matters. A cabin at the lake sounds like the perfect place to spend a good old-fashioned Thanksgiving."

"It does sound relaxing," I agreed.

"I have a couple of new holiday-themed mysteries that arrived today. They won't even officially be on sale until after Thanksgiving, but I nabbed us a couple. I'll grab one for your mom as well. Maybe we can all read the same book and then hold a discussion."

"Sounds like a lot of work for a vacation."

"It'll be fun."

I groaned. While Bree found reading relaxing, I much preferred a video game. Not that I never read. I did. But I was a slow reader, and I didn't want the extra burden of reading so many pages a day in order to participate in a discussion.

Bree and I chatted for a few more minutes, then Tilly and I continued on our way. I wanted to take a minute to chat with everyone as I dropped off the mail so I could remind them that they'd have a substitute mail carrier the following week, but I also wanted to finish my route at a decent time. Tony was coming over for dinner and gaming tonight, and I wanted to get home in time to clean up a bit before he arrived. Not that it mattered all that much if I didn't manage to get my laundry tucked away in the hamper. I was sure Tony loved me, messy home and all.

"Afternoon, Brick," I said to local pub owner Brick Brannigan. "You have mail today." I held up two envelopes. Brick didn't have mail more than once or sometimes twice a week, so I didn't come in every day as I did with the other merchants on Main.

Brick reached out a hand. "Thanks. I've been waiting for a letter from my uncle, who's coming into town next week. I still don't know what day to expect him."

"Why don't you just text or email him?"

"He doesn't do cell phones or texts or emails. He's currently on a road trip, so I can't call him on his landline. He said he'd drop me a letter once he'd narrowed down to a specific date." Brick ripped open one of the envelopes. He took a minute to read whatever was handwritten on the enclosed piece of paper. "It looks like he'll be here Wednesday."

"That's good." I smiled. "He'll be with you for Thanksgiving."

Brick frowned. "Yeah, but then I'll have to cook. Maybe I'll just take him to your mom's place."

"She's closing the restaurant for the whole week. I think pretty much everyone's closed on Thanksgiving Day. Maybe you can buy a precooked turkey from the meat market and add a few sides. Actually, you might be able to buy the sides precooked as well."

"Good idea. I'll do that."

I'd turned to leave when Jordan Westlake walked in. Jordan was new to White Eagle. He'd moved to town the previous month after inheriting an old house he was in the process of renovating. It was huge, so the renovation was going to take some time, but I couldn't wait to see what he'd done with the place so far.

"Afternoon, Tess," Jordan greeted.

"Afternoon, Jordan. How's the renovation going?"

"Pretty well. The kitchen is just about done, as is one of the bathrooms on the first floor. I have a long way to go, but I finally feel like the place is functional."

"I can't wait to see what you've done with the house. It really does have so much potential, and when we discussed your plans, they sounded wonderful."

"It's been a labor of love, although love isn't the only emotion I've felt for the place."

"That's understandable after everything that happened there. I heard you went to visit Hannah and Houston last week." Hannah and Houston Harrington were twins and Jordan's cousins. Sort of. It's a long story, but basically, Hannah and Houston spent two years living in the house Jordan now owned after their father dumped them, along with their three other siblings, in White Eagle while he went on with his life in San Francisco. The legend surrounding the house had been both creepy and incomplete, so Tony and I, along with Mike and Bree, had helped Jordan track down the truth, which led to the information that the two youngest of the Harrington siblings hadn't died as teens as everyone had thought after all.

Jordan nodded. "I did go to visit them."

"And how was it?"

"Strange, but nice. I felt a little weird to be the one who ended up with the house, even though I'm not a Harrington by blood. It does seem the house should have gone to one or both of them, but they assured me that they were fine with my having it because neither had any intention of returning to it or White Eagle ever again."

I understood that. Their time in White Eagle had been its own kind of hell.

Jordan continued. "I'm happy to be able to confirm that both Hannah and Houston have gone on to have fairly normal and happy lives. They most definitely had a rough start, but once they got out from under their father's control they seem to have blossomed."

"I'm really happy to hear that. Any news on Hillary?" Hillary was Hannah and Houston's older sister. She'd faked her own disappearance and run away long before they did.

"I haven't had any luck tracking her down. I have a feeling the twins know where she's been, and whether she's still alive, but it was very apparent that, while they were interested in meeting me, the subject of their sister was off the table."

"If they do know where she's been, and if she's still alive, I imagine they're protecting her. It's a complicated situation."

"It really is. I have plans to see them again. I think we can be a family of sorts. I'm hoping over time they'll be willing to fill in the blanks about Hillary."

"I hope so. It would be nice to have the rest of the story."

"It really would. I'm heading to San Francisco next week to spend Thanksgiving with family, but I'd love to get together with you and Tony when I get back."

"Call me and we'll set up a date. Maybe dinner."

"Sounds good, as long as we go out or you're planning to do the cooking. I'm afraid that isn't one of my talents."

"Tony's an excellent cook. I'll invite Mike and Bree too, and we'll meet up at his place. Feel free to bring a date, or if you don't know anyone, I can invite someone to even things out."

"I have someone in mind," Jordan said. "I'll call you when I get back."

I said goodbye to Brick and continued on my route. It looked like Tony was going to have to live with socks and underwear on the floor. I should have done the picking up that morning, but I'd gotten a late start and really did think I'd have time to get to it this afternoon. I sighed. Oh well; there were worse things than a messy cabin.

I was just finishing up when I got a call from Brady Baker, the veterinarian in town. About a year ago, Brady had taken over for his uncle, who had been the only vet in White Eagle for a long time. In addition to running the veterinary clinic, Brady owned and operated the only animal shelter in town.

"Oh good, I caught you," Brady said. "I wanted to ask if you could come to the clinic early tomorrow morning."

"Sure. I can do that. Is something up?" I opened the door to my Jeep and Tilly jumped inside. I tossed my empty mailbag on the back seat.

"There's a man coming by at seven thirty to look at three of our dogs. He adopts dogs from shelters around the country and trains them for FEMA. He's in our area and heard about our shelter. He was impressed with our personalized training program and asked if I thought we had any dogs with potential. I want to show him Gracie, Bosley, and Sammy. I hoped you could be here to help me with the demonstration."

"I'm happy to help out. What a great opportunity." Gracie was a golden lab, Bosley a German shepherd, and Sammy a Border collie mix. All had received basic training and were young and healthy. I considered them to have real potential for specialized training as search-and-rescue dogs.

"Great. I'll see you in the morning. And bring Tilly. She has a calming effect on the shelter dogs."

By the time I dropped off my empty mailbag and chatted with my coworker for a few minutes at the post office, it was a good thirty minutes past the time Tony had told me he'd be by. I'd given him a key to my cabin and knew he'd let himself in, but I'd hoped to be home early enough not to keep him waiting. Our lives had certainly changed since we'd admitted our love for each other. I felt like the world around me was somehow brighter, richer, and happier. I'm not sure why I hadn't realized sooner that Tony was the guy for me, but now that I'd opened my eyes, I planned to never let him go.

Tony's truck was in the drive when I pulled up. He'd turned on the white twinkle lights he'd strung all around my property, making it look like a magical fairyland. My heart smiled as I climbed out of my Jeep and let Tilly out behind me. "Titan's here," I said to Tilly, referring to Tony's dog.

Tilly must have figured that out on her own because she ran toward the front door the minute I let her out of the Jeep. Tilly loved Titan, and it was obvious the feeling was mutual.

Tony opened the door and stepped out onto the front deck. I walked into his arms and sighed with happiness when they closed around me. Tony had been working hard to finish up a project he'd contracted for and wanted to have completed before we left for our trip, so I hadn't seen him since the previous Monday morning, when he'd brought me back to my cabin after we'd spent the weekend at his place.

"I've missed you," Tony said into my ear.

"And I've missed you. Did you finish your project?"

"I did. And I don't have anything else until after the first of the year, so from this point forward, I'm all yours."

"That sounds pretty darn good to me."

Tony took a step back and we turned toward the front door. "I was about to start dinner," he informed me.

"It can wait. I need to change out of my uniform and I thought maybe you could help me."

Tony grinned. "You know I like to be helpful."

******

A long time later, Tony started dinner, while I logged onto my computer to check my emails. I didn't normally get a lot, but I didn't have time to check them at all during the day, so I'd settled into the routine of checking all my messages when I got home each evening. I supposed missing an evening wouldn't be the end of the world, but ever since Tony and I had begun searching for my father, I felt compelled to check to see if I'd received anything that might be connected to it in some way. Not that I ever had. The only email we'd received that was even remotely connected to it was one Tony had received about my mother. Still, although the clues leading to my dad's disappearance were slim, a girl could dream.

I thought about the information we'd been able to uncover as I waited for the computer to boot up. The whole thing had started shortly after my dad died, or I should say supposedly died, fourteen years ago. I was fourteen when I was told my dad had died in a fiery truck accident while driving the cross-country route he'd been working most of my life. A year later, I was nosing around in the attic of the house Mike and I lived in with our mother and found a letter hidden in a book that I believed at the time to be encrypted. Believing it could somehow provide an answer to the questions I'd been having since my father's death, I'd decided to try to break the code. After dozens of failed attempts, I had no choice but to enlist Tony's help. As it turned out, the letter hadn't been encrypted at all, but that search had led us to uncover some anomalies in my father's death, which was what I'd suspected all along. We decided to keep our search to ourselves as we continued to dig. We'd come up totally empty until this past December, when Tony found a photo of my dad standing in front of a building that had been constructed three years after his supposed death. Two months after that, Tony found a photo of my dad in a minimart. At the time, the photo had been only two years old.

Since then, we'd gotten other hits that suggested my dad was not only alive but something of a world traveler. We hadn't been able to find mention of a Grant Thomas since his death, so we were working under the assumption that he'd changed his name. The most recent clue was sent to Tony just three weeks ago. This photo of my dad looked as if it had been taken in Eastern Europe and appeared to come to him in real time, meaning that unless it was a trick of some sort, my dad was alive as of three weeks ago. Of course, Tony had warned me the photo could be a fake, and we should consider any evidence we dug up suspect until proven otherwise.

The other interesting thing Tony had uncovered was that Grant Walton Thomas didn't seem to exist before 1981. As far as I knew, he was born on April 12, 1957, in St. Louis, Missouri, but according to Tony, he didn't have a paper trail of any sort until shortly before he married my mother.

In addition to the photos of my dad that Tony had dug up along the way, someone had sent him a photo of my mom standing on a bridge in Norway. I later learned that was taken while she was on vacation in Europe before she ever met my father. The really odd thing was, in the photo she's standing on the same bridge as the man we thought could have been my father at an earlier age. I spoke to Mom about it, and she assured me that, while they did look alike, Jared Collins, the man on the bridge, and my father weren't the same man.

The more we learned about my father's past and disappearance, the more confused I became. I wondered who had sent Tony the photo of my mom and why. It wasn't as if we were doing a facial recognition search on her image, so why had the photo turned up in his in-box?

"Because I've barely spoken to you in a week, I wanted to ask if you had any new hits on my dad," I asked Tony after I'd checked my handful of emails— mostly ads—and logged off.

Tony paused from chopping garlic. "I haven't had any additional hits with the facial recognition program, but I've done some digging to see if I can turn up anything connected to your dad's time at Timberland Lake. When you told me that your mom wanted us to spend the week at the place your dad took his annual fishing trip, I decided to look for any references I might be able to uncover."

"Makes sense."

"Did your mom happen to say why she wanted to visit that particular lake?"

I shook my head. "I thought it odd that she wanted to go there after all these years when she first brought it up, but I didn't want to make a big deal out of it so I didn't say anything."

"Do you think it might have something to do with your asking her about her trip to Europe last month?"

I frowned. "Maybe. I guess that would explain why she's suddenly interested in visiting a place my dad spent so much time during their marriage. Bree wondered if Mom missed Dad and was looking to make a connection of some sort by visiting a place he seemed to love so much."

"Do you think she's right? Do you think she's missing your dad?"

"I don't think so. That doesn't feel right to me. She loved my dad, but it wasn't the stuff of fairy tales. They actually didn't spend a lot of time together. He was on the road most of the time, and even when he wasn't working, he would go fishing or hunting. And yes, she was sad when he died, but I don't remember her falling into a deep depression. In fact, it seemed to me that she grieved quickly and then got on with her life in a fairly efficient manner. To suggest she'd be missing him all these years later would be odd. I suspect she might just want to do something different this year. Aunt Ruthie is going to be out of town with her son and new granddaughter. Mom might just have been feeling at loose ends."

Tony tossed the garlic he'd chopped into a pan with diced onions and olive oil, then began to stir. "I guess that might be all there is going on. Still, it seems like a good opportunity for us to dig up a new clue. I don't think we should be obvious about it, but I do think we should plan to do a little sleuthing while we're at the lake. If your dad went up there every year, I'd be willing to bet there are people who live in the area who might remember him."

I popped a piece of the bread Tony had buttered in preparation for broiling into my mouth. "That's a good idea. The fact that he returned to the same lake every year with such faithfulness almost makes me think he was meeting someone there."

"Did he ever mention seeing anyone?" Tony asked.

"No. He just said he needed time to think," I answered. "That never made sense to me because he spent most of his time driving back and forth across the country alone. Seems like he had plenty of time to think then. But my mom seemed fine with it, so who was I to question his motives?"

"My research turned up the fact that the man who owns and rents the cabins on the lake has been doing it for over thirty years. He must have known your dad. And if he was meeting someone there, he should know that as well. As soon as we get settled, we'll head over to the rental office and have a chat with the guy."

I frowned as a thought occurred to me. "If my dad is still alive, which we seem to have good reason to suspect, do you think he continued to go up to the lake even after he supposedly died?"

Tony tossed some shrimp into the sauté. "I wouldn't think he would have. I mean, he was supposed to be dead. It seems like he'd go out of his way to avoid any place where he was known in his old life."

"Yeah. I guess you're right. But how funny would it be to run into him by the lake or at the local pub?"

Books by Kathi Daley

Come for the murder, stay for the romance

Zoe Donovan Cozy Mystery:

Halloween Hijinks
The Trouble With Turkeys
Christmas Crazy
Cupid's Curse
Big Bunny Bump-off
Beach Blanket Barbie
Maui Madness
Derby Divas
Haunted Hamlet
Turkeys, Tuxes, and Tabbies
Christmas Cozy
Alaskan Alliance
Matrimony Meltdown
Soul Surrender
Heavenly Honeymoon
Hopscotch Homicide
Ghostly Graveyard
Santa Sleuth
Shamrock Shenanigans
Kitten Kaboodle
Costume Catastrophe
Candy Cane Caper
Holiday Hangover
Easter Escapade
Camp Carter
Trick or Treason
Reindeer Roundup

Hippity Hoppity Homicide
Firework Fiasco
Henderson House
Holiday Hostage – *December 2018*

Zimmerman Academy The New Normal
Zimmerman Academy New Beginnings
Ashton Falls Cozy Cookbook

Tj Jensen Paradise Lake Mysteries by Henery Press:

Pumpkins in Paradise
Snowmen in Paradise
Bikinis in Paradise
Christmas in Paradise
Puppies in Paradise
Halloween in Paradise
Treasure in Paradise
Fireworks in Paradise
Beaches in Paradise
Turkeys in Paradise – *Fall 2019*

Whales and Tails Cozy Mystery:

Romeow and Juliet
The Mad Catter
Grimm's Furry Tail
Much Ado About Felines
Legend of Tabby Hollow
Cat of Christmas Past
A Tale of Two Tabbies
The Great Catsby
Count Catula

The Cat of Christmas Present
A Winter's Tail
The Taming of the Tabby
Frankencat
The Cat of Christmas Future
Farewell to Felines
A Whisker in Time
The Catsgiving Feast – *November 2018*

Writers' Retreat Mystery:

First Case
Second Look
Third Strike
Fourth Victim
Fifth Night
Sixth Cabin
Seventh Chapter

Rescue Alaska Paranormal Mystery:

Finding Justice
Finding Answers
Finding Courage
Finding Christmas – *December 2018*

A Tess and Tilly Mystery:

The Christmas Letter
The Valentine Mystery
The Mother's Day Mishap
The Halloween House
The Thanksgiving Trip – *October 2018*

Haunting by the Sea:

Homecoming by the Sea
Secrets by the Sea
Missing by the Sea
Christmas by the Sea – *December 2018*

Sand and Sea Hawaiian Mystery:

Murder at Dolphin Bay
Murder at Sunrise Beach
Murder at the Witching Hour
Murder at Christmas
Murder at Turtle Cove
Murder at Water's Edge
Murder at Midnight

Seacliff High Mystery:

The Secret
The Curse
The Relic
The Conspiracy
The Grudge
The Shadow
The Haunting

Road to Christmas Romance:

Road to Christmas Past

USA Today best-selling author Kathi Daley lives in beautiful Lake Tahoe with her husband Ken. When she isn't writing, she likes spending time hiking the miles of desolate trails surrounding her home. She has authored more than seventy-five books in eight series, including Zoe Donovan Cozy Mysteries, Whales and Tails Island Mysteries, Sand and Sea Hawaiian Mysteries, Tj Jensen Paradise Lake Series, Writers' Retreat Southern Seashore Mysteries, Rescue Alaska Paranormal Mysteries, and Seacliff High Teen Mysteries. Find out more about her books at **www.kathidaley.com**

Stay up-to-date:

Newsletter, *The Daley Weekly*
http://eepurl.com/NRPDf
Webpage – **www.kathidaley.com**
Facebook at Kathi Daley Books –
www.facebook.com/kathidaleybooks
Kathi Daley Books Group Page –
https://www.facebook.com/groups/569578823146850/
E-mail – **kathidaley@kathidaley.com**
Twitter at Kathi Daley@kathidaley –
https://twitter.com/kathidaley
Amazon Author Page –
https://www.amazon.com/author/kathidaley
BookBub –
https://www.bookbub.com/authors/kathi-daley

CPSIA information can be obtained
at www.ICGtesting.com
Printed in the USA
BVHW041826200921
617146BV00023B/310

9 781723 239069